THE CASE

The Unbolted Lightning

By
Thomas Brace Haughey

ACCENT BOOKS
Denver, Colorado

ACCENT BOOKS

A division of Accent Publications, Inc.
12100 West Sixth Avenue
P.O. Box 15337
Denver, Colorado 80215

Library of Congress Catalog Card Number 86-70276

ISBN 0-89636-212-4

DEDICATION

To Ernie Braund, Smitty, Sartain, and my other friends and former co-workers at the Library of Congress. Little did they know that the seminarian employed there once as a part-timer would come back to haunt them years later by dropping a murder on their doorsteps.

CONTENTS

1
SPRING STORMS CAN KILL

It was one of those picture postcard days. The usual London drizzle had sputtered out by mid-morning. Skies were clear. The air, washed clean of motor car fumes, sported a fresh, flower-blossom scent that had succumbed only moments before to the aroma of bread baking in the brownstone across the way. Spring had at last arrived! As I gazed out the living room window, I decided I'd like nothing better than to take a stroll down Baker Street, listen for birds, and wave friendly greetings to our neighbors. Mrs. Kelsey would no doubt be out tending her shrubs or walking that ancient terrier her late husband had given her. The pensioner, Bottomley, would be sitting on his stoop with his nose stuffed into a book. He always read as I passed and never grunted more than a word or two my way. Yes, it would be great fun to tour the neighborhood again in the sunshine. In my mind's eye I could see Bottomley turn to his wife after I passed.

"Maude, there goes tha' blighter John Taylor again. Abou' time, if you arsk me. He's pudgier than ever. Some detective! How's 'e chase down billies? I wonder. It must be tha' Weston fellow, 'is partner, wha' does all the running. And 'im the brains, too! Though you'd neva' know it by the looks o' 'im. A regular goateed Maypole and wearing those ridiculous sweaters. That Geoffrey Weston! He puts on airs 'e does! What with opening up that Sleuths, Ltd. business right on Baker Street ta trade on 'is ancestor's name. You'd think that Holmes chap was 'is bloomin' father instead o' some dead relative. If only they weren't so obsessed wi' religion . . . ."

I shook my head and bailed out of my woolgathering.

Perhaps I should have visualized a less waspish character or injected a trifle smaller dose of realism into my daydream. Enforced inactivity plus the half stone I'd gained during the winter must be getting to me.

"The boredom's affecting both of us," Weston said from behind me.

I jumped involuntarily and turned away from the window to face my disconcertingly clairvoyant partner. I realized even as I turned that he must have been studying me for some time over the rim of his morning paper. During the incredibly long gap between cases, he'd become rather addicted to observation games, or as he put it, he'd been "honing his skills and staying sharp." But as he "stayed sharp," I'd noticed his fingernails growing progressively shorter and duller.

"So," I responded, "I remain as transparent as ever. Would you care to join me?"

"On a walk through the neighborhood?" Weston folded the paper and laid it down beside him on the sofa. "If my symptoms of cabin fever are as pronounced as yours, I fancy I'd better. Honestly, John, as cut and dried as that case was two months ago, I'm glad we took it. Nearly two months without work is bad enough. I'd hate it to have been longer."

"You and me, too," I agreed, "but that Grumwald strangling was a little more of a challenge than you seem to remember. I doubt the Yard, unassisted, would have hit on the notion that trained dolphins were smuggling drugs across the channel."

Geoff bit his lip and glanced briefly at the ceiling.

"Perhaps you're right. But any remedy we effected was so temporary. As long as England's pink and blue haired offspring strut down the street in peacock clothing looking for a thrill, the drugs will be there. And people will die. They just die a little slower when we dry up a source, that's all."

"Which," I reminded him, "is why our last fee went to support street missionaries who try to convert young hooligans."

8

Weston nodded.

"True. And I wish I were out on the streets right now working alongside them."

"And," I added, "getting stabbed in the back. Let's face it, you're a might too recognizable as the Yard's ally."

Instead of answering, my partner reached down the neck of his sweater and extracted a bag of peanuts from his shirt pocket. It was obvious he felt his fame to be rather a straight jacket. After fumbling unsuccessfully to open the bag with dulled fingernails, he ripped it open with his teeth and popped a few nuts into his mouth.

"You are," I persisted, "about the closest thing to a textbook workaholic I've ever seen. You'd be the world's worst street missionary and you know it. Flinging down devastating intellectual arguments on the untrained and illiterate who wouldn't understand a word you said. You have a calling, and you're the best in the world at it. But when you're forced to rest, you can't."

"Which brings us back," Weston noted sardonically, "to *your* cabin fever. You've had three dates a week with *Miss Albey*, went skiing in Switzerland with her brother, and know every exhibit at the British Museum by heart, but you're just as impatient for work as I am. Admit it now, aren't you?"

"Almost," I conceded, "but not quite. I, at least, can stop working and be impatient. You simply substitute other, less satisfying, jobs while you brood. Look around you . . . at that spotless laboratory table in the corner . . . at the orderly bookshelves . . . and the uncluttered coffee table. There isn't so much as an untended cup or a decent pile of books anywhere in the room. Even Gladstone has noticed the unnatural neatness. Yesterday he meowed around my legs for half an hour complaining that all his best perches had evaporated under your unrelenting assault."

"No big problem," Weston assured me. "Cats are adaptable."

I arched my eyebrows. "More than some people I know! Speaking of dating, which you were a moment ago—when

9

was the last time *you* stepped out with a lady?" I raised my hands in a stop gesture. "No, don't bother to tell me. It was with Paloma Guerrero, the Presidente's daughter after that incident in Mexico City. And that was two years ago. Two years! A few letters, my friend, don't take the place of a flesh and blood courtship or even of face-to-face conversation. There are some intelligent, really spiritual women at church who wouldn't find you too disagreeable. One or two are even rather pretty. Or are you bent on playing out some Holmsian family custom, worshipping your own private Irene Adler from afar and building a wall between yourself and the fairer sex?"

Weston looked almost as though he'd been struck, and I was rather sorry I'd said that. Then he sighed and gave himself over to devouring a second handful of nuts.

"You are," he said between chews, "very fortunate to have a friend like Jane. And you're doubly so not to be quite so much in the limelight as I am."

"Meaning?"

"Meaning that I get shot at just a little too often. And any woman I showed public affection for would become a target, too." He forced a smile. "Besides which, what young lady in her right mind would want an irascible curmudgeon like me? Look at me, John. I'm too tall, too thin, too lacking in the social graces . . . . " He paused to brush salt off his goatee. "And, as you pointed out a moment ago, I'm too much the intellectual. Women, I've noticed, prefer well-mannered, disgustingly gallant, medium-tall airheads who play rugby or football and bear the distinct appearance of having been photographed in Hollywood or sculpted on Mount Olympus."

I shook my head and leaned back against the windowsill.

"You surprise me, Geoff. Right now you really do sound like your great uncle."

"How so?"

"In the chauvinistic way you stereotype over fifty percent of the global population."

"And," Weston continued for me, "you're going to point

10

out examples of my error, starting with all the past queens of England."

"Something like that," I agreed.

He scowled and eased himself to his feet. "What say we go on that stroll now, and I'll fill you in on my philosophy of women while we . . . . "

The jangling of our telephone broke his train of thought.

"I'll get that," Geoff volunteered. He strode quickly to the hallway and fairly pounced on the receiver.

"Hallo. Sleuths Limited for service unlimited. Yes . . . Yes, this is Weston. Just a second. I'll put you on the horn so my associate, Mr. Taylor, can hear." He punched a button and dropped the receiver in its cradle. Static crackled from the speaker as I hurried closer. Then a woman's voice overpowered the background hiss. Her accent was very distinctly American, midwestern and well modulated.

"Mr. Weston, I'm Cathleen Strong, Senator Strong's wife. My husband's been murdered, and I'd like to retain you to find his killer."

"Could you," my partner prompted, "give us a few of the details—location, date, method, possible motives, and the like?"

"Certainly. But first I want your promise that you'll hear me out. I'm afraid that both the local police and the FBI think I'm crazy."

Geoff couldn't suppress a smile. "An opinion, madam, which the local constabulary has often expressed about me as well. Please proceed."

Her voice had the peculiarly hollow twang that one often hears in transatlantic long distance calls.

"I'll take that for a promise not to hang up. Mr. Weston, two days ago my husband was apparently struck by lightning while standing on the steps outside the Library of Congress's main building. I don't believe for one moment, however, that it was an accident."

"And what's your reason," I interjected, "for being suspicious?"

11

There was a startled pause. "Oh, you must be the associate. Simply, Mr. Taylor, that Senator William Kidd of Texas . . . he's chairman of the Armed Services Committee on which my husband also serves—served . . . Senator Kidd was struck by a lightning bolt from the same thunderstorm not twenty minutes later."

"And," I prompted, "he died also?"

"Very definitely. On the ninth tee of the Bethesda Chevy Chase Country Club. At least seven people, caddies and players, saw him hit. Death was instantaneous."

Weston, obviously deep in thought, stroked his goatee.

"And the enormity of the coincidence," he mused, "leads you to infer . . . ."

"That it's not coincidence. Absolutely. Mr. Weston, both Jim and Senator Kidd were opposed to selling—or should I say practically giving—certain out-of-date military hardware to Mexico. A crucial vote on the proposal was to come next week, and with their opposition it would never have gotten out of committee. Now it looks like it will. I believe that was the motive and that the murders were cleverly disguised as accidental so as not to influence other members' votes."

Geoff picked up a booklet from the telephone table and began leafing through airline schedules.

"The motive," my partner observed as he continued turning pages, "is just a might thin unless there's over-whelming support for the measure throughout the legislative branch and it's unlikely the President would veto."

"I'm afraid," our caller admitted, "that the vote would be rather close even in the Senate. But at the moment I don't rule out horse trading, dirty tricks, and even bribery to push the measure through both houses. Anyone who'd kill to insure its reaching the floor would be capable of anything."

"Except," I pointed out rather skeptically, "that you're starting to argue in a circle. The motive proves the deaths weren't coincidence, but then the deaths are used to bolster up a weak motive. Couldn't the whole . . . ."

"What my partner means," Weston cut in, "is that we'll

need to conduct an investigation to confirm or disprove your suspicions."

Mrs. Strong's response was clipped. "Understood. At least you'll try. My husband spoke highly of your reputation. I'm prepared to pay a retainer of twenty thousand American dollars. In addition, as soon as the estate's settled, I'll pay any reasonable bill of expenses you might submit. If you succeed in bringing my husband's murderer to justice, there'll be an additional payment of $200,000 in currency or, if you prefer, tax free bonds. Give me the name of your bank and I'll arrange an electronic fund transfer of the retainer immediately. Naturally I don't expect you to book passage solely on the basis of a phone call."

"Naturally," Weston agreed. "We bank at Barclay's, Oxford Street Branch. Let me see . . . . " He ran his finger down the schedule listing. "The next Concorde takes off at half past noon our time, which gives us just under two hours to pack our bags, draw out funds for the trip, and make it to the airport. That's assuming, of course, that the flight isn't booked. What's your Washington address?"

"4308 Bradley Lane, Bethesda. I'm so close to the country club I could have seen the bolt that killed Senator Kidd if I'd been home. The quickest way to get here, if you land at National, would be to take the Metro to the Bethesda or Chevy Chase exit."

"Quite." Weston jotted down the address. "What's your phone number?"

"301-555-1712."

"I've got it. We'll be seeing you shortly. Oh, one last thing. Don't let the mortician bury your husband's body before we get there."

"He won't," she assured him. "In fact, I didn't even allow embalming. The body's been frozen pending your examination. It's at the Stout Funeral Home."

Weston nodded approvingly. "Excellent. Goodbye, then, for now. I'll give you a call before we barge in on you."

"Goodbye . . . and thank you."

Weston cut off the connection and began dialing a local number.

"John," he ordered without so much as glancing my way, "throw some clothes into a couple of bags while I arrange for reservations. No guns, of course. As non-residents, I fancy we won't qualify for a permit or a purchase."

"Nor even," I surmised, "for a kind word from the local police commissioner."

"Hallo," Geoff spoke into the receiver. "I'm wondering if you have a couple of seats open on flight number 705 to . . . "

I hurried down the hall and began going through both bedrooms, stuffing the contents of wardrobe and dresser alike into two far-too-small suitcases. My hands fairly flew but experience caused me to check labels on my own clothing and choose winter sizes while I aimed at spring styles. It felt good to be rushing about again trying to make a deadline. If only I was more comfortable with the particulars of this case! There were one or two details that were decidedly troubling. By the time I returned to the living room, Geoff had finished calling both the airport and a taxi company and had added a few items to the portable laboratory we kept suitcased for such occasions. A strident honking outside announced the arrival of one of London's mad coachmen, so we lugged our baggage out into the fresh air, locked the deadbolt, and turned away from the dim brownstone's interior to embark on yet another adventure.

The motorcar sped south on Baker Street, then skidded left and entered the two-way traffic of Oxford. The driver shifted capably through the gears and we were still accelerating as we careened past the bustling Bond Street underground station toward Oxford Circus and, beyond that, the bank. I settled more comfortably into my seat and fastened the safety belt. Weston was more accurately settling into discomfort since his knees pressed into the back of the driver's seat and he had to hold his head in a slight but perpetual duck to avoid the roof. He glanced anxiously at his

14

watch, an action which took little effort since his head was already pointed in the right direction.

"Don't worry," I volunteered, "we'll make it all right. But I'm not sure we should have taken on this job at all."

Weston shifted his weight again. "These tin cans," he confided with stoic resignation, "are probably called 'compacts' because they represent some designer's pact with the devil."

"Or perhaps," I joined in, "because they're intended to squash everyone down to that mythical state known as 'average.' But you're trying to avoid responding to me. I've struck a nerve, haven't I?"

Weston extracted a pen from his pocket and began spinning it between his fingers like some miniature baton. His lips compressed for just an instant.

"Yes," he conceded, "I guess you could say that. You know, of course, that Paloma's last letter said she'd be accompanying her father to Washington when he came to lobby for that military arms package. Since I'm a friend of both father and daughter, it might appear rather as a conflict of interest to represent the family of someone allegedly killed for opposing the aid they're seeking. But, oh bother, that very friendship gives me an open door to investigate the international angle."

"And that," I prodded, "is the full reason for your unease?"

Weston stopped batoning. "But of course. What other reason . . . "

"Simply that the evidence seems awfully flimsy to me that there has been any crime at all. Perhaps it's only wishful thinking on your part. Or . . . "

We both lurched forward as the cabbie slammed on the brakes and swerved around a motorcar that had stopped to sightsee.

"Perhaps," Geoff finished dourly as he righted himself, "the boss is just jumping at a chance to travel, expenses paid, to America and renew acquaintance with his modern-day

'Irene Adler.' That's what you're thinking, isn't it?"

"Yes," I admitted, "I guess it is. Not that I'd impugn your character, but I think you may have rationalized a bit. After all, what do we have here but a possible coincidence? It's unlikely, I'll grant you that, that two officials would die in the same storm, but far more unusual things have actually happened."

"True. But the location of Senator Strong's death has everything to do with our taking the case."

"Then you admit a trip to Washington was . . . "

"Absolutely immaterial!" Geoff related icily. "No, John, I'm referring to the Senator being struck directly in front of the Library of Congress. As you may know, buildings generally afford a sixty degree cone of protection from lightning. An edifice that high would most probably shield all the area between the outer wall and the street. Perhaps not quite that far, but close to it. In other words, lightning would tend to arc toward the building and miss entirely those hardy souls strolling outside. In the case of the Library of Congress, that happy event is even more certain. As I remember, the building sports a solid copper dome held aloft by a steel skeletal structure buried within its granite walls. It is, in other words, an exceptionally well-grounded, natural, lightning rod. Lightning striking anywhere close would most certainly curve and hit the dome."

"Then . . . "

He nodded. "The Senator was most assuredly murdered. I don't know how, as yet, but we'll have a go at finding out. That close to the U.S. Capitol, it's hardly likely someone could have helicoptered a laser weapon aloft, but there are some other tantalizing possibilities for us to explore. First I'd like to . . . "

Geoff didn't have a chance to finish. A huge beer lorry came dashing in front of us from Regency Street. Our driver slammed on the brakes in a futile gesture and I ducked, covered my head, and closed my eyes. I felt the terrific, screaming jolt of the collision followed by a dizzying spin as

16

we careened across Oxford Circus and up onto the sidewalk. By the time Weston and I unfolded ourselves and peered out what was left of the windshield, a geyser of steam had enveloped the front bonnet. The cabbie, who appeared merely shaken up, cursed with a skill which bespoke long practice, unfastened his seatbelt and staggered outside to inspect the damage. I ruefully touched an egg-shaped bump on my forehead that probably wouldn't have been there had I buckled up. Weston, who seemed unscathed, reached over and switched off the taxi meter.

"John," he observed with a sigh, "let's pull what's left of our equipment from the boot before this wreck blows up. It looks as though we'll have to take a later flight."

2

THE DEATH OF SLEUTHS LTD.

As the glass doors of Washington National Airport automatically slid aside for us and we stepped out into the morning sunshine, I must admit that my brain felt rather numb. Not even the fresh, after-shower air scented with just the hint of cherry blossoms could revive me. Yesterday, after replacing everything breakable in our equipment bag and dropping by the bank, we'd managed to book a reservation on a lumbering, wide-bodied jet that struggled into Kennedy just late enough so we missed the evening's last connecting flight to Washington. Even the usual assemblage of robed flower peddlers had gone home, so there wasn't so much as a good argument available to keep matters interesting.

We were reduced to nodding our heads in half slumber for four hours while wishing that someone had had the foresight to install headrests on our plastic seats' short backs. The whole ordeal was rather like a KGB interrogation. When we'd reached semi-delirium and our muscles were cramped into pretzled knots, the horn had summoned us to gate twelve for boarding. Later, after takeoff, our flight attendant had handed us a bag of peanuts instead of breakfast. I'd arrived at National Airport stiff, bleary-eyed and famished.

Weston paused briefly to gaze about the parking lot. He set his bag down briefly on the sidewalk, stretched and breathed deeply.

"Marvelous! John, you were absolutely right. There's nothing nicer than a brisk walk on a cool, breezy morning. I'd prefer we skip the taxis and try that elevated tram station over there, what hey." He paused to ponder a brochure he'd picked up in the terminal. "After all, there isn't a whole lot we can do until Mrs. Strong arrives home and answers her phone. An examination of the crime scene seems a good preliminary move, and I notice the train runs right by the Library of Congress."

I gently touched the welt on my head and, despite any mental numbness, winced.

"You'll get no argument from me on that point. If I never get into another taxi, it'll be too soon. But do you think they'll allow carry-on luggage aboard? The underground in Mexico City didn't."

"If not," Weston reassured, "why build a station at the airport? Come on. The worst that can happen is they'll turn us back."

So he hefted his suitcase again and we strolled right on by the assortment of yellow and checkered cabs lined up expectantly awaiting fares.

In less than five minutes we found ourselves standing on hexagonal clay tiles in a cement walled anteroom, confronting a thoroughly incomprehensible ticket-vending machine. The only "official" handy was industriously pushing a broom down the entrance corridor, but we did find a fare and destination list on an unmanned information booth. Since there was no bill changer about, we stuffed dollars into the vendor and experimented by pressing buttons until tickets and a few dimes popped out. Then we challenged the turnstiles, which were actually slide stiles, by inserting our hard-won tickets into the slots. We were nearly chewed to death as the slide stiles opened and then closed suddenly on us before we'd stepped completely through. It was evidently a "no no" to pause to retrieve the tickets which reappeared for our future use from yet another slot. As we escaped the monster's clutches and strode toward the escalator to the platform, I glanced backward and only then noticed a travelers' instruction sign hanging inconspicuously in a corner.

"These Yanks," Weston commented philosophically as we rode upward, "appear a might thoughtless concerning

19

tourists, but they certainly enjoy their high technology."

"They do, indeed," I commented dryly. "Let's hope that human conductors rather than semiconductors guide the trains. I don't think I'm quite ready yet to ride a guided missile."

"Perfectly harmless," Weston quipped. "It's the misguided missiles one has to worry about." Just then we reached the top of the stairs and stepped off. "My, the cars certainly are pretty, aren't they? Shining aluminum with ample observation windows. We should get a nice view of the District whenever we're above ground." He paused to consult his brochure. "According to the map, we're at the end of the blue line which meanders a bit but does eventually pass by the Library of Congress. The yellow, which intersects this at the Pentagon, is more direct, but I think we've experienced enough layovers today already. The blue it is, all the way!"

I heartily agreed. "Righto! Say, you haven't got any more peanuts, have you? I'm absolutely starving, and if we're going on the grand tour . . . . "

Weston patted his pockets as we walked along and handed me a bag just as we stepped into the car. It was then that I saw the sign.

Smoking, eating, drinking, spitting, littering, playing radios without earphones, carrying animals, flammable liquids or dangerous articles punishable by fine or imprisonment.

"It seems," I observed ruefully, "that we shouldn't have forgotten to pray before starting this trip."

Weston chuckled good naturedly. "I prayed for both of us during the layover. The Lord must have His reasons."

The trip was uneventful and, for the most part, underground. We descended for the Pentagon, surfaced briefly at Arlington Cemetery, and then plunged under the Potomac amidst ear popping and furious swallowing by the small coterie of passengers. Although it was rush hour, the cars were only half full, so our baggage proved no problem at all. After passing through the business district, we disembarked and rode an escalator from a dim, waffle-walled cement cavern to daylight. Two blocks and a bag of peanuts later we stood on the sidewalk in front of one of the world's more imposing buildings.

It was evident that the Library of Congress had been built roughly during England's Victorian era. Out front foot-thick stone railings rimmed three levels of patios and flanked wide stone stairways. Green copper lampposts atop the railings sported leaves and scrolls and were topped by clusters of white glass globes under spiked crowns. A more traditional post still had a hole under its glass cage through which a lamplighter had no doubt inserted his pole before the days of electrification. The building itself was just as grand and ornate as its surroundings. A circular drive passed directly under the main entrance stairway, presumably so that patrons could disembark under the arches and enter the ground floor without getting wet on rainy days. Those that wished to walk the stairs, however, were treated to quite a sight. The building was fairly alive with gargoyles mounted over arched windows, bas-relief maidens draped around the entrance arches and, on the first balcony, busts in front of windows over doors. I say the first balcony because there was yet another above it supported nearly the length of the building by massive Corinthian columns ascending from the balcony floor. And even above that, at the roof's edge, another stone railing hinted at occasional strolls around the dome which was nearly invisible from my angle.

"My word," Weston breathed with a touch of awe, "I don't believe I've ever seen such a busy building. Not even Bellas Artes, the concert hall in Mexico City, holds a candle to it. And the pillars! Do you notice there are ornamental columns in the entrance arches and on the balcony? Even on that second balcony where it juts out, there are columns in the shape of people holding up a section of roof! What a sniper's delight. Anyone could hide behind any one of a hundred obstructions, pop out and fire a laser beam or high voltage weapon with only a small chance of being detected."

"I'm touched," I commented dryly, "by your sense of artistic appreciation. Where should we begin the investigation?"

My partner began to slowly make a complete turn, watching with keen intensity everything about him.

"Those large maples and pines on the Capitol grounds could hide a man aloft. And look at the garbage lorries blocking every entrance. Either the two houses of Congress produce an inordinate amount of red tape that needs hauling, or there's fear some suicide bomber will try to ram the Capitol Building. We'll have to check the back of that truck over there to make sure it's remained empty or filled with weights, or whatever."

He continued turning. "The Supreme Court's a little too far away and doesn't provide a good angle for shooting, so we can ignore it. Every ledge of the library will, of course, have to be searched for evidence either of a sniper or a spotter. But first, let's toddle over to the upper patio and see if we can find the actual location where the Senator was struck."

As we began climbing stairs, I noticed a man in a blue uniform stepping out of the main entrance.

"That colored gentleman up there," I suggested, "looks like a guard. Perhaps he can give us some information."

"The preferred adjective in this country," Weston corrected, "is, I believe, 'black'. And, yes, you're absolutely right. Let's make his acquaintance."

The closer we got to the guard, the more impressive he seemed. His close-clipped curly hair and mustache were streaked with just enough gray to lend an aura of distinction, but his lithe, well-muscled frame bespoke strength. He was, furthermore, dapper to the nines. I could have sliced my finger on his pants crease!

"Excuse me, sir," Weston spoke loudly to catch his attention, "I was wondering if you might help us. My associate and I have just arrived from London, and . . . well, we heard some chap was struck by lightning on these steps, and we'd like to know exactly where he was standing when it happened."

The guard broke into a broad grin as he focused his attention on us. When he spoke, his accent was smooth middle American.

"So you fellas are finally here. I must say it's about time."

"About time for what?" I inquired.

"For the investigation. A man like that must have had an insurance policy in the millions. You're from Lloyds, aren't you?"

"As a matter of fact," I corrected him, "we're from Sleuths Ltd. of Baker Street. But we have been retained to conduct an investigation."

He shrugged at the news.

"Same difference. The name's Charlie Hansen, if you need it for the record." He chuckled. "For that matter, it is even if you don't."

Weston made a show of slipping a note pad out of his pocket and writing down the name.

"Is that spelled with an 'en' or an 'on'?"

"An 'en' like the highway or the patriot."

Geoff crossed out the word and rewrote it.

"Now, Charlie, could you tell us what you know about the death."

"I'd be delighted. I was the guard on duty at the entrance desk that morning. You see, we check handbags and briefcases when anybody leaves to make sure books don't go for a walk without a loan slip."

"By that morning," I broke in, "you mean what?"

"Excuse me. Monday morning at eleven thirty-three."

Weston frowned as he scribbled the time. "How can you be so exact?"

"Because I have to log the time whenever I leave my post."

"And," Geoff concluded, "you left your post."

"I sure did. There was a tremendous explosion of thunder out front that shook the windows and like to made me jump out of my seat. Then I heard a man screaming and yelling for help. So I ran outside. Senator Strong was lying over by that picnic table." He gestured toward an orange one by a potted shrub. "And the man who'd done the screaming was leaning over him giving CPR. It didn't do any good, though. He was as dead as a mackerel. Anyway, I ran back inside lickety-split and called the paramedics. They were here in five minutes, but couldn't revive him. I understand he was pronounced DOA."

"You wouldn't," Weston prodded, "happen to know the name of the other gentleman, would you?"

"Why certainly. It was Senator Throckingham. The two had just walked by my desk on their way to lunch. Leastways they mentioned a new luncheon special at the Senate cafeteria."

"I see. Charlie, you wouldn't be able to arrange matters, would you, so I could get a look at the roof and the front balconies?"

For the first time since we'd met him, the guard lost some of his affable self-assurance and seemed puzzled.

"I guess I could get it cleared at the office, but why would you want to look there?"

"Let me answer your question," Geoff responded, "with a couple of my own. Was Senator Throckingham or Senator Strong by any chance carrying a briefcase when he left?"

"Yes, they both were."

"And did you open them for examination?"

"Of course not. They're Senators, and this is the Library of *Congress.* We exist to serve their needs."

Weston snapped his fingers.

"Precisely. Now just suppose Senator Throckingham wanted to kill Senator Strong. He carries a portable defibrilator—the kind hospitals use for restarting hearts—in his briefcase. A confederate on the roof watches for witnesses and when he sees the coast is clear, tosses a

24

concussion grenade over the side. The resultant flash and explosion simulate lightning and momentarily disorient the victim. Throckingham, without opening the valise, pulls disguised paddles from their receptacles, jolts Strong's heart into silence, and then simulates CPR for your benefit so no real help will be provided until it's too late."

The guard struck his hand to his forehead in exasperation.

"But that's absurd. Senator Throckingham's reputation is absolutely...."

"Absurd, perhaps, but not impossible," Geoff's eyes narrowed ever so slightly. "When I give my report, I have to rule out every possibility. The best service you can do for the senator right now is to provide me the opportunity to rule out any such theory."

Charlie Hansen stiffened.

"Then that's exactly what I'll do. Come with me to the guards' office please, and we'll make the arrangements."

He started down some side steps, evidently intending to enter the building through the gound floor archway. Before following, Weston spoke with me in subdued tones.

"John, be a good chap and investigate the area around here and across the street. If I finish before you, I'll come lend a hand."

I nodded. "Understood."

As my partner left his luggage in my care and hurried to catch up with the guard, I shifted my attention to the area around the picnic table. Sliding a magnifying lens out of my suit coat pocket, I got down on my hands and knees and began an inch-by-inch study of the yard-square patio tiles. The red clay surface was, I discovered, reasonably clean due to the recent shower. At one point near the table, however, I did manage to scrape some melted rubber and a char mark from the paving. The poor blighter must have been wearing leather soled shoes with rubber heels when it happened. As I got up to have a look at the table itself, I happened to glance upward and noticed Geoff on the upper balcony with his nose almost touching the railing. He must be looking for marks made by some sort of gun mount. Evidently he wasn't particularly convinced by that theory he'd propounded. Nor was I. The melted rubber, if left by the victim, argued against a low voltage electrocution. Neither had I, so far, seen any shredded wadding left by a concussion grenade.

The table and benches proved to be quite ordinary. There wasn't anything hidden, so far as I could tell, in the tubular frame. An examination of the potted shrub was equally fruitless. I went back onto my hands and knees and little by little widened the circle of my search. After an hour I gave up in disgust. Aside from a candy wrapper and a couple of pennies, the area was utterly bare. I transferred my efforts to the other side of the street.

The garbage lorry was the open-topped kind and proved to be nearly full of debris. I almost fell in while making my inspection. There were enough empty boxes in it that someone could have excavated a corner for a private residence, but I saw no sign that it had actually been done. The close-clipped grass of the Capitol grounds likewise thwarted my efforts at detection. If any clues had fallen to earth, they'd long before settled down between the blades or been carted away by one of the squirrels that now followed me about begging for tidbits I didn't have to offer. The maples were, of course, another matter. The tender bark of the trunks should have shown scars from any recent climbs, but didn't.

My investigation turned up nothing. Since Weston hadn't as yet returned, I retraced my steps to the patio, retrieved our bags, and trudged through the front entrance. Inside I was met with all the grandeur of a concert hall. Gold leaf high up on the elaborately engraved ceiling set off stained glass scenes in the skylights. Marble staircases with sculpted marble bannisters ascended on both sides of the huge anteroom to an encircling gallery which provided yet further opportunities for the display of statuary and Grecian columns. The ceiling above the gallery was, however, decidedly Ottoman in character, featuring arch after arch inlaid with mosaic designs and symbols. I hardly had time to gawk before spotting my lanky partner fairly skipping down the righthand staircase toward me and seeming totally out of place in his sweater, slacks and tennies. Geoff waved while still a good thirty feet away. His voice boomed out and echoed to the discomfiture of library patrons.

"What a marvelous place, old bean! It has everything but sliding bookcases and hidden passageways, and I wouldn't even rule those out completely! Marvelous, but with nary a clue in sight! How were the gleanings outside?"

I put my finger to my lips in a plea for quiet and started up the stairs. As I did, Geoff paused to await me on the landing.

"Unfortunately," I responded in more subdued tones, "they're rather slim. But a couple of melted rubber blotches and some char marks did turn up. Real lightning still seems quite likely as the culprit."

"I see." Geoff considered the matter even as he accepted the return of his suitcase. "What about the lorry?"

"Filled with trash, but a possible hiding place. However, if I could look inside without being spotted and arrested on suspicion of planting explosives, then someone else could have jumped in undetected. The boxes and bags near the top don't seem, though, to have been crushed."

"Then that's all for it here." My partner snapped his fingers, "except that it might be most interesting to find out what Strong was reading the day he died."

I nodded. "It jolly well might, at that. Where's the Congressional Reading Room?"

"I ran across it during my wanderings," Weston confided. "Follow me."

He turned on his heels and began ascending the stairs with such enthusiasm that I found myself struggling to catch up. The man seemed positively invigorated by the thrill of the hunt.

At the top of the stairs we turned right and headed toward a side corridor that looked like it was straight out of the Sun

King's summer palace. Seven flowered bas-relief pillars on each side supported gilded, gingerbread arches that spanned not only the corridor itself but also every side door and window. Oil painted virgins on the ceiling looked down at geometric designs in the mosaic floor. A mahogany sign standing in the middle of the corridor entrance declared "No Admittance. Members of Congress and their staffs only." Weston, however, paused before reaching that spot to read one of several quotations carved into the main gallery's wall.

It is the mind that makes the man, and our vigor is in our immortal soul.

"A good observation," I volunteered. "It almost sounds like a theologian defining man's soul as his eternal personality."

Weston nodded in agreement. "At the least it declares that humans have one and that it counts for something. Quite an admission on a government building, wouldn't you say? I wonder if Supreme Court justices ever pass by and take notice."

"If they visit," I observed, "their attention's probably more drawn to the gingerbread and glitter up ahead."

"No doubt."

He turned suddenly and brushed on past the "No Admittance" sign. I followed suit a little more tentatively and couldn't help noticing how loudly my shoes clacked on the tile floor as we advanced toward mahogany double doors at the corridor's far end. Another free-standing sign announced "Congressional Reading Room" but omitted the injunction against entering. Possibly due to that omission, Weston didn't even hesitate, but pulled the doors wide and stepped in. Since I'd already passed into a forbidden area, there wasn't much I could do but take up the rear. The room was unoccupied except for a bifocaled, balding gentleman seated at one of the brass-lamped study tables and an elderly lady sorting call slips from behind a massive desk. We walked toward her with a confident briskness that I didn't at all feel.

"Madam," my partner introduced himself, "Cathleen Strong, the late senator's wife, has sent us to tie up certain loose ends. We'd very much appreciate a list of any books he had out on loan at the time of his death."

The silver-haired librarian seemed distinctly puzzled as she looked up from her work. "But I don't understand, young man. I asked the loan division to tube that information to the Russell Building fully two days ago."

My partner fairly beamed. "Wonderful. Then there shouldn't be any trouble at all in having your computer run off a duplicate letter. My, this does speed things up. We'll also need a look at any volumes he might have had on reserve for reading here. And, oh yes, if you have any record of what he actually looked at the day of his death, that should prove useful, too."

The woman glanced uncertainly from one to the other of us and drummed her fingers on the desk.

"I don't know," she responded at last. "I'd like to help, but this is terribly irregular. For all I know you two could be reporters digging for a story. I don't remember you being on the senator's staff. Could you show me some identification?"

"Better than that," Weston interrupted, "you can call Mrs. Strong yourself and she'll vouch for us. Her home number's 555-1712, but please feel free to look it up in your own files. Credentials can, after all, be forged or borrowed, and we wouldn't want to jeopardize your job."

Obviously relieved at being offered a safe course of action, she flashed us her first smile since we'd entered.

"Why, of course, I can do that. And I do have the number around here somewhere." Her fingers started thumbing through a circular telephone file on the desk. "The senator," she confided, "requested a special search a few months ago for a misshelved.... Well, at any rate, he left his home number so we could let him know the moment it was found." Her fingers stopped and she leaned forward to read. "Ah, here it is, 555-1712. You're absolutely right."

She dialed nine for an outside line and began pains-takingly adding numbers, checking her card after each dial.

"Our names," I remarked conversationally, "are John Taylor and Geoffrey Weston. We . . . . "

"Please young man!" She seemed to startle herself with her own outburst, then lowered her voice to a near whisper. "Please don't talk while I'm dialing. You'll make me lose my place."

"Oh, I'm terribly sorry. I . . . . "

I allowed my words to fade out, and Geoff and I waited impatiently in silence while the librarian finished dialing. She put the receiver to her ear and we could just make out the faint sound of ringing. Six . . . seven . . . click . . .

"Mrs. Strong, this is Sady Billingsly down at the library. Yes. It's good to hear from you again, too. That surplus book auction really went over the top, didn't it? We couldn't have done it without your help. The reason I'm calling, though, is that there are two gentlemen here who say you sent them. You didn't send anybody." Her expression hardened as she looked at us. "I see. Then I'm sorry that . . . . "

"Just a moment," I cut in, "she only gave us general directions. Tell her our names."

"Excuse me," she continued into the mouthpiece. "The men insist . . . No, I haven't seen them before, and one doesn't even have a suit on. They say they're a Mr. Taylor and a Mr. Weston. No! You don't say. In a plane crash. Of course. Just a minute."

She cupped her hand over the mouthpiece and addressed us with cold finality. "Mrs. Strong informs me that both John Taylor and Geoffrey Weston were killed yesterday. Give me your real names and your reason for coming or I'm afraid I'll have to call for a guard and have you arrested."

"Madam," Weston responded dourly, "I assure you that, as your Mark Twain once said, 'the reports of my death are greatly exaggerated.' Give me the phone a moment and I think I can straighten this up."

30

Wordlessly Sady held out the receiver for him and he snatched it up.

"Mrs. Strong," Geoff spoke crisply, "I have your retainer of $20,000 which you transferred to Barclay's of Oxford Street. We missed the Concorde. Yes, I'm rather glad we did, too. No survivors. How... Do they have any idea what caused the explosion? Yes, that certainly is terrible. It's a wonder to me why the 'Islamic Holy War' is always so quick to boast of committing atrocities. Look, it's really not important that we come see you right now, but we would like you to stay put so we can call whenever we need a ticket into some restricted area. Yes, I'll put her back on."

He handed the phone to the librarian.

"Yes," she spoke into the receiver, "it's Sady again. Uh huh, uh huh. They are. Well, it certainly bends the rules a bit if they're not staffers. They want to see your husband's records. No, I guess we can do it. Yes, I see. Thank you, and goodbye."

Sady directed her attention to us. "If you'll wait a moment, I can get the Loan Division records out of the computer for you. I'm sorry, the senator didn't leave anything here on reserve. Congressmen seldom do, unless it's something they all want at the same time and we have to limit their access."

"What about," I reminded her, "books or articles he might have read on his last day?"

She folded her hands in front of her. "I'm afraid I can't help you with that. We don't keep a record of books delivered, and slips marked 'not on shelf' are returned to the reader. Senator Strong either threw them in the trash or took them with him."

"You mentioned," Geoff prompted, "that the gentleman sometimes asked for special searches. Might he have made such a request on *Monday*?"

Her face brightened. "Oh, how silly of me. Of course he did. I remember it distinctly. Now let me see."

She swiveled her chair sideways and began typing into a computer terminal. After a brief interval a printer whirred to life and a sheet of paper ejected line by line from its top. When it stopped, she ripped the sheet out and handed it to Geoff.

"There's what you want. The last book is the one under search. The others are loan division."

I nodded as Weston scanned the list.

"Thanks ever so much for your help," Geoff said. He frowned as he continued reading. "How could we, I wonder, go about finding one of the library annex buildings?"

The librarian reverted to the bored inflection which so often accompanies memorized instructions. "Take the rear elevator to the sub-basement and follow the tunnel to the annex. Watch the signs and you won't get lost."

"Thank you," Weston repeated. He handed me the sheet and turned to leave. "We'll do that."

Once again it was all I could do to keep up with my partner as he headed for the door. We'd reached the hallway, in fact, before I had a chance to peek at the list. Then I let out a low whistle.

"What an eclectic reading pattern! *Spinoffs of Space Technology; Extinction of the Stickleback; Psychotic Diseases: Symptoms and Cures; Handouts with Strings; The Case for Supply Side Economics; The Case of the Frozen Scream,* one of our own investigations! That must be how Mrs. Strong knew to call us. My word, the last one on the list's a might suggestive, isn't it? *The Limitations of Biological Warfare?*"

"It certainly is. Congress does occasionally vote on such matters, but it's highly suggestive. Right now, though, let's concentrate on getting out of here while we're still alive."

"But I don't understand. Surely we're not . . . . "

"John," he rattled off crisply, "a lady asked us to investigate a murder. We told her *over the telephone* what plane we'd leave on. It was blown up by people who *claimed* to be Arab terrorists. Now we've told the same woman at the same address over the same phone where we are right now. What's the worst case scenario?"

"But you couldn't mean . . . . "

He nodded grimly.

"I rather suspect her phone was tapped and that there's an assassin either on the way or standing outside this very moment. That's why we leave from the back of the Annex building. I only hope they can't mobilize enough operatives fast enough to cover all the exits. We appear to have fallen into a pit of invisible vipers and it just might be a bit sticky getting out alive!"

"Then," I suggested, "let's speed up a little. I believe I've gotten my second wind."

3
THE PRINCE AND PAUPERS

Senator Throckingham's outer office tried hard to give the impression of style, hard work, and solid dependability without opulence. Just enough papers were scattered across the receptionist's desk. The outline plaque of the State of Alabama hanging on the wall was just massive enough. Silk flowers in blues, reds, and yellows lent a touch of color to the somber mahogany paneling which seemed just a might out of place in a structure as new as the Dirksen Building. We'd signed the guest book and were awaiting an audience—or was it interview—with the senator while his secretary, a blond in her mid twenties prepared some complimentary passes to the House and Senate galleries for us.

"It feels good," I reflected with a sigh as I sank even deeper into the sofa, "to at last be rid of our luggage and reduced to carrying a mere camera bag. What an answer to prayers to find an apartment for let right across from the Shakespeare Library."

"Whose prayers?" Weston asked with just a hint of merriment.

"Why mine, from the moment you foisted your suitcase on me and I had to grow a third eye to keep the lot from being stolen while I was scaling garbage trucks. And a good thing we're traveling light now. It would have taken us a half hour to get through the metal detectors downstairs."

"Garbage truck," Geoff corrected, "in the singular. And, yes, the security here is rather strict. But if I were brought in as a consultant, I think I'd make some changes."

"For example?" I prompted.

"For one thing, I'd station sniffer dogs at every door. Did

you notice how readily transistor radios are passed through? One of them could easily disguise a detonator. And plastic explosives, of course, are non-metallic and would currently be undetectable. Another thing I'd do is . . . . "

"Mista' Weston," the secretary interrupted our subdued conversation, "the Senator will see ya'll now." She stepped over to a door on the right and opened it for us. "Heah are yo' passes." She flashed a smile designed to dazzle. "Ah hope ya enjoy yo' stay in Washington."

"Why thank you, madam." Weston took the proffered tickets. "I'm sure we will."

He returned her smile and we walked into the senator's inner sanctum which was similar to his outer sanctum except that the desk confronting us was three sizes bigger and occupied by a Churchillian type complete with cigar, double chin, and paunch. Our host stood to greet us and seemed most imposing flanked by eagle-headed poles flying the American and Confederate-like Alabama flags. He extended his hand in greeting and boomed at us in a friendly voice used to addressing large campaign crowds.

"Mr. Weston, Mr. Taylor. So good to meet ya. Ah couldn't believe it when Mrs. Quincy told me you'd stopped by." He let go of my hand after giving it a generous pump and gestured toward the chairs behind us. "Have a seat. It's been one of ma' ambitions to shake yo' hand evah since ya saved that satellite of ours from bein' taken ovah. We're all in your debt, suh."

Weston and I both eased onto leather padded chairs.

"Why thank you, Senator," Geoff responded. "But that was a fairly simple matter."

"Call me Billy Bob, the name ma' friends use. No, it wasn't at all easy, but ah appreciate yo' modesty. Now tell me what brings you heah?"

"Well, Billy . . . Bob," my partner began, "we're investigating Senator Strong's death, and we're not entirely convinced at this point that it was a simple case of a lightning strike. I understand you actually saw the event."

Billy Bob turned toward his office intercom and pushed a button.

"Mrs. Quincy, please hold all ma' calls for the next fifteen minutes."

"Yes, Senator."

He redirected his attention to us.

"What Ah saw . . . " He paused to rub his chin. "What Ah saw was the most horrifyin' thing Ah've eva' witnessed, and Ah've served in two wars. Jimbo wasn't more'n two steps ahead o' me when he commenced ta glowin', and then there was a blue-white flash that nearly blinded me. Ah thank God for rubba-soled shoes because as it was Ah got jolted right off ma' feet. And there was this wall o' hot air. When Ah got up, Jimbo was just lyin' there with a wicked burn ova' his forehead. Ah tried ma' best ta revive him, but he was beyond hope."

"I take it," Geoff prompted, "you were walking away from the building at the time and facing the Capitol."

"We were. We'd planned ta have lunch togetha' in the Senate dining room and talk ova' some compaign matters."

"Such as?" I inquired.

Senator Throckingham folded his hands on the desk.

"Such as," he answered with a touch of regret, "how James Strong was goin' ta be the next president of the U-nited States. He would have won, too. We had the perfect plan."

"Which," Geoff attempted to burst his bubble, "would have been copied by every other candidate if it actually was perfect."

"No, no, it wouldn't have. That was part of the plan's perfection. May ah speak with you for a moment off the record?"

"We know how to keep confidences," I assured him. "What you say will go no further than this room."

"Thank you." He paused to open a box of cigars and offered them to us. "Care fo' a smoke?"

"No thank you," Weston declined. "We don't smoke."

The Senator nodded gravely.

"Glad ta heah it. If Alabama weren't a tobacca growin' state, Ah think Ah'd quit myself. But don't tell that ta the tobacca farmers. Every one of 'um claims the Surgeon General's wrong. No, I take that back. One farma told me cigarettes were deadly but that all his crop was somehow goin' ta be ground up and fed ta goats and cows to deworm them. Imagine that!" He closed the box. "As Ah was sayin', our plan was perfect because it was so radical there wasn't anotha' man on Capitol Hill who'd have dared try it.

"Gentlemen, when this great nation was founded, the statesmen of that era knew that the people themselves were the greatest threat ta sound government. Greed, suh, had toppled the Roman republic, and it might well destroy us. So they wrote checks against the people into the Constitution along with all the otha' checks. That's why we have an electoral college. And that's why we used ta have a Senate elected by the state legislatures. Our country, when it began, was really a collection of sovereign states with a Senate represented by delegates who were insulated from the people and whose job it was ta ratify treaties and keep the House from goin' on mad spendin' sprees. Since the early 1900s, howeva', senators have been directly elected, too, and have followed the House's lead in promisin' voters the moon in orda ta get elected. Speakin' bluntly, yo' folks must realize that this country's in bad shape financially."

"I've heard rumors to that effect," Geoff acknowledged. "But what's that got to do with anything?"

"Simply this. We conservatives have always been at a disadvantage. We say 'spend less' while the liberals offa' generous bribes out of the public coffers, all in the name of humanity, of course. We say 'save;' they say 'spend.' We say 'cut;' they say 'add.' We say 'don't do;' they say 'do.' Who would y'all vote for? Until a few years ago conservatives had gotten scarcer 'n hen's teeth around this neck of the woods. Then taxes and unemployment got so high 'supply siders' were able ta come along and offa' lower taxes, less inflation, and mo' jobs as a counta' bribe. But we've been afraid ta dismantle the welfare state, even if it's only the liberal politicians that get well and the people who pay the fare. What Jim and Ah were gonna do was ta finally take it apart— ta appeal ta people's greed in a way that'd cause them ta help us rip it down."

"Go on," Weston interposed, "we're all ears."

"Well, suh, we have millions of people on welfare, jest eekin' out a livin' from day ta day, but afraid ta take a low payin' job because they'll lose benefits. We have otha' thousands administerin' the program and afraid they'll lose their own high payin' jobs if it succeeds in gettin' people outa' poverty. And we have millions in the middle class who hate the taxes but are afraid they'll be outa' work themselves someday.

"What we were goin' ta do in the campaign was ta promise ta do away with welfare entirely and in its place give away ta heads-of-households now in the program fifty thousand tax free dolla's with no strings attached. The person could use the money ta start a business, buy a home, or invest in bonds and get as much in yearly interest as the government now gives in assistance. The difference is that the interest income would be *on top of* any salary he might earn. There wouldn't be restrictions. And the government could fire its costly bureaucracy and trim billions of dolla's from the yearly budget. We'd break the poverty cycle and actually save money doin' it. The initial payment, itself, only represents the welfare budget for four years, including overhead."

"What about," I wondered aloud, "the chaps who misspend their money or who lose their jobs after the new program goes into effect? And why wouldn't everyone quit work to get the free money?"

Throckingham smiled. "Let me answer that last question first. Of course we'd back date the eligibility ta those on the rolls before the political campaign began. Otherwise we might cause a stampede. We'd also offa' financial counselin' ta all the newly affluent. And we'd also institute a program of 'workfare' which would allow the futa' indigents ta run child care centahs, build bridges and the like fo' minimum wage. That way even unmarried motha's would have time ta work by havin' cheap child care available. Those who refused ta work wouldn't eat. That's in the Bible, ya know. We'd still provide, of course, fo' the physically handicapped or convalescent, but by makin' a one-time payment that could be invested, we'd encourage the handicapped who can ta work doin' whateva they can."

"And what do you do," I ventured, "for the children of an unmarried woman who refuses to work?"

Billy Bob shrugged. "Ah suppose we'd offa' clothes along with some food ta be eaten in the child care centa's."

"And if it was winter?" Weston queried.

"Then we might have ta take action against the motha' for neglect and place the children in a warm fosta' home at least temporarily. But rememba' that the problems ya bring up would only affect a relatively small group of people. Millions would still have escaped the poverty cycle and would be workin' and creatin' jobs for otha's. Taxes would go way down, and government would get smaller."

"And your man," Geoff concluded, "would buy enough votes to be swept into office. He'd be elected through perfectly legal bribery."

Billy Bob beamed like the Cheshire cat. "Very well put . . . off the record, of course. As Ah said, the plan was perfect. The ultra liberals neva' could have endured it because it smashes fifty years of their pet projects ta smithereens. We'd have won hands down."

"I have to admit," Weston observed thoughtfully, "that I'm intrigued by the notion, particularly since it wouldn't foster laziness as so many government projects unintention-ally end up doing. But I believe there's one crucial error in the scheme. The program should be announced after the election, not before. You see, you've spoiled the whole thing by your own selfish motives and by appealing to the avarice of voters. You've made your utopian scheme the most

39

Machiavellian philanthropy since Caligula gave senatorial voting rights to his horse. Your mixed motives produce what seems to me the most loveless gratuity since Judas Iscariot cast down his silver before the priests. Are you really trying to help mankind or simply gain power? And please don't say you want to gain power to help mankind, because you injure man by the methods you'd use to get that power. It's unspeakably evil to pander to the worst in man, whether by running a lottery to finance education, supporting wholesale abortions for women's 'convenience,' or offering a bribe to gain office."

Instead of becoming angry as I half expected, Billy Bob continued smiling in a most genuine manner. Political life must have thickened his skin to elephantine toughness.

"Ya'll would have loved Jimbo," he reminisced. "He sounded just like you. Our luncheons were neva' dull, Ah tell ya. He'd rant n' rave, tellin' me how people would vote fo' him because they wanted ta help their neighba's. What nonsense! They'd shoot their neighba's ta get in front of them in the hand-out line. But Jim's sincerity made him all the mo' effective sellin' the plan. He was a regula' evangelist. Ah, on the otha' hand, am a pragmatist. Ah firmly believe that politics is the art of the possible. Even Jim probably realized deep down he needed someone like me ta represent him in the smoke-filled rooms. As one of those 'born-again' religious fanatics, though, he neva' would have admitted it." Throckingham paused to blow cigar fumes in our faces. "Idealists get eaten alive in this city unless they're backed by wheela'-deala's who'll do the compromisin' and horse tradin' for them. Anybody who really wants a second term ends up panderin' ta the people. That's what direct election of senators does. Of course, back when state legislatures made the appointments, there were still city machines dictatin' some of the choices. Howeva' the numba' of folks linin' their pockets was smalla', so budgets were smalla'."

Weston shook his head incredulously. "No wonder," he concluded, "Pontius Pilate, when face to face with Christ, couldn't think of a better question than 'What is truth?' He must have made nearly as many moral compromises during his career as you have. He actually lost his faith in absolutes. I pity you, Senator, because you haven't realized that the ends don't justify the means. The ends are, rather, an ethical extension of the means. You quote Scripture to justify starving the lazy, but there's another verse which says that if we do evil that good may come of it, our condemnation is just. The means, sir, are all important. The idealist who seeks election by appealing to the electorate's sense of justice and generosity and whose motive for running is to stave off governmental bankruptcy and break the poverty cycle demonstrates personal nobility. That would seem to be Jim. The cynic, on the other hand, who seeks the same ultimate goals *in order to consolidate power* and by consciously appealing to men's baser instincts is another animal entirely."

"And that," Throckingham finished, "would be me. But it wouldn't make one percentage point difference in the polls."

"No, it wouldn't," Weston conceded. "Voters aren't particularly adept at reading minds. Say, now that Senator Strong's out of the picture, you aren't planning to make a run for the presidency yourself, are you?"

Billy Bob's gaze was unwavering, "So, the detective comes back to the supposed crime seekin' motives. Ah assure you, Mr. Weston, that Ah've no aspirations fo' the presidency. Nor does ma' pragmatism extend ta murdah. There hasn't eva' been a president from Alabama and there probably neva' will. Jimbo had a chance of the party faithful selectin' him because he was from a large state and didn't speak with a regional accent. The most Ah could eva' hope fo' is a vice-presidential nomination ta balance the ticket, and Ah'd prefa' to stay in the Senate where there's more real powa' ta serve my constituency."

"I believe you mean that," Geoff concluded, "and I certainly have appreciated your candor."

"Ah've said what Ah've said because Ah believe ya need

ta know what's goin' on around here ta find Jimbo's killa' if there is one. And Ah'm well enough acquainted with you ta know that if ya think ya smell a skunk in the woodpile, it's probably there. The flash looked like lightnin' ta me, but then Ah was right busy fallin' down at the time."

"You mentioned," I prompted, "that Senator Strong glowed an instant before being struck. Could you describe that a little more exactly?"

"Well, suh, he was surrounded by a kind of blue-white corona about...maybe half an inch thick."

"And uniform in intensity?"

"So far as Ah could tell. Ya have ta realize it all happened so quick...."

"No doubt about that," Weston agreed. "Could you pull some strings to find out if any weather or defense satellite might have photographed the event?"

His eyes fairly twinkled.

"Ah *am* on the Armed Services Committee. But are ya sure you want help from an old wheela'-deala'?"

"As long," Weston assured him, "as you throw your weight around but not your money."

Throckingham chuckled a full-throated chuckle just short of a belly laugh.

"Ah like you, Weston. Ya speak yo' mind and don't back down."

"It comes with the territory," Geoff responded. "You kiss babies. I catch murderers."

"Or," the senator amended, "ya try to. In this case Ah wish you well, and Ah'll do anything Ah can ta help."

Geoff eyed the senator shrewdly. "There is one additional thing you can do which might be of assistance. There are probably good reasons for keeping the campaign coalition you've been building a secret, but I'd appreciate a list of Strong's backers."

"Ta be used in confidence?"

"To be used only for purposes of investigation. I won't, as you say, 'leak' to the press. You can trust us on that. We're a couple of—what were your words?—'born-again religious fanatics' just like your friend."

Throckingham appraised each of us in turn.

"You'll have yo' list, but it'll take a while ta put togetha'. If ya like, Ah'll even mark the two or three most likely ta run in Jimbo's place."

"Very decent of you."

"But if it becomes public, Ah'll deny Ah know anythin' about it."

Geoff couldn't suppress a smile. "I somehow suspected that. Senator, when you compile the names and addresses, would it be too much bother to have an aid trot on over and slip it under our door? We're headquartered just a couple blocks from here . . . at 217 East Capital Street, Apartment 1B."

Throckingham slid a pen out of its desk top holder and jotted the direction down.

"No, no botha' at all. What's yo' telephone numba' so I can give y'all a call if Ah find out somethin' from the Pentagon?"

Geoff pulled a slip of paper from his trousers pocket.

"It's 555-1766. I'd appreciate it, though, if you'd keep both the address and the number confidential. We'd like to limit access to those who'll help forward the investigation."

Throckingham stood up in silent signal that the interview was over.

"Ah quite undastand. Our home phone's unlisted, too. If it wasn't, Ah'd be listenin' ta crackpots all night long."

I reached over the desk to shake the man's hand. "It's been a pleasure, Senator, to chat with you. We'd both like to thank you for giving us so much time from your busy schedule."

"Indeed we would," my partner echoed as he in turn stretched his own hand forward. "About that list . . . Will we find the late Senator Kidd's name on it, I wonder?"

Throckingham held the handshake an extra second.

"No, suh, ya won't. Ah'm afraid my distinguished colleague, although strong on defense, was a might liberal in matta's of the economy."

"I see. Well, thank you again for your trouble."

"Don't mention it. Always glad ta be of service."

The senator escorted us to his office doorway and bade us a final "good day" as we walked across plush maroon carpet toward the outer exit. We'd hardly stepped into the hallway when he turned to his secretary.

"Savannah, would ya please step in heah for a few minutes ta take dictation. And get me the file on...."

The door clicked closed and squeezed off the rest of his words. I remembered belatedly that I should have left him a gospel booklet. Then I realized he probably already had a pile of them, courtesy of the victim.

4
IF THE SHOE FITS

I didn't see very much of the city that afternoon. We took the underground tram from the Dirksen Building to the Capitol, walked through the rotunda while gawking like tourists at the painting, "The Baptism of Pocahontas," and descended to a second tram which we rode to the House side of the Hill. There we briefly surfaced to hail a taxi to L'Enfant Plaza where we entered the labyrinth of the city underground and boarded a train for Bethesda. A stalker would have had to be a troglodyte to track us! So far as we could tell we weren't being followed, though I did notice a curious glance or two as we worked our way through the Capitol crowds. Perhaps it was my imagination. There's nothing, after all, like an invisible saboteur to turn every stranger's face into an assassin's mask.

The gusty breeze against our faces felt decidedly bracing as we emerged from our subterranean world onto a suburban Maryland sidewalk. As I stepped out from under the entrance canopy, however, I couldn't resist a worried glance at the thunderheads building overhead. Since we'd brought neither greatcoat nor umbrella, we stood a good chance of testing our "sanforized" labels within the hour.

"There's a rent-a-car agency down that sidestreet," I ventured. "Perhaps now's the time to grab a bite at one of the burger stands and toddle over for some transportation. The center city's one thing, but we're going to walk ourselves ragged traipsing about Montgomery County."

Weston picked up the pace and started across the street toward a fast food franchise.

"Don't I know it," he agreed matter-of-factly as we dodged

traffic. "But we can't risk a motorcar. Habitually used vehicles make too easy a bomb target. I don't fancy turning on and blowing up. We'll just have to hail a cab if distances prove too great. Otherwise we walk." We stepped onto the opposite curb. "After all, I distinctly recall your wanting to take a turn around the neighborhood yesterday."

"Around the neighborhood, yes," I retorted. "Not around the world."

We dined on bagged fried potatoes and flounder burgers served in styrofoam boxes—America's answer to fish and chips. Perhaps it was on account of my ravenous hunger, but the meal didn't seem bad, actually. My spirits had decidedly risen as we walked the few blocks to the mortuary.

"You know," I commented as we strolled past a skyscraper shopping plaza, "your idea will never catch on."

"And which one might that be?"

"Candidates announcing their campaign platform *after* their election. It would make for rather dull campaigns, don't you think?"

My partner chuckled. "Yes, yes, I guess it would."

"Of course," I bantered, "one could always run with the promise of 'continued humility.'"

Weston's eyes fairly twinkled. "Some Christian virtues *are* rather rare in politics, aren't they. Say, isn't that a hearse parked two blocks down? That brick manor house must be the . . . ."

Thunder reverberated from the buildings about us as the first large drops of rain pelted our shoulders. We stopped talking and, by mutual consent, ran for all we were worth while trying to avoid the shoppers ahead of us who, for the most part, scurried to huddle under store overhangs. Within the first fifty yards we had clear sailing as my partner forged out to a substantial lead. I set my eyes on the funeral home's pillared porch and vowed not to slacken stride before reaching its shelter. Isolated drops gave way to sheeting torrents, and we were both thoroughly soaked as I huffed and puffed up the steps to meet Geoff who was already standing by the front door. I noticed between gasps that he was breathing a might heavily himself. When we'd regained a measure of composure, I pushed the bell button and listened to the melodious chiming which issued from deep inside. A moment later the oak-paneled door opened outward to reveal a well-manicured, surprisingly youthful gentleman every wit as staid and proper as the colonial-style manor that framed him. Uncertain as to the reason for our visit, he managed a smile which sought to be warm and friendly but just a might melancholic.

"May I help you..." he noticed our drowned rat appearance, "... gentlemen?"

"Why yes." I stuck my hand in my pocket and presented him with a somewhat limp business card. "Cathleen Strong has sent us to examine her husband's body."

His expression noticeably brightened. "It's about time. Now maybe we can schedule the funeral."

"A distinct possibility." Geoff acknowledged.

"If you'll follow me, I'll take you to the preparation room."

Without waiting for us to reply, he turned and started down the hallway. The door closed automatically behind us as we stepped inside and hurried to catch up.

The "preparation room" turned out to be a basement chamber that fairly glistened with stainless steel appointments. We approached the far wall which sported what looked like a restaurant freezer fitted with two banks of square doors. The funeral director yanked one of the handles and pulled out a long, drawer-like pallet on which the victim's body rested with the traditional name tag tied to his big toe. I could see even at a glance that burning had been extensive on the head and feet.

Geoff slid the magnifier from his trousers' pocket and rubbed it dry with lens paper from his wallet.

"John, you examine the upper torso while I have a look at the extremities. Take particular note of any scarring, even if it seems unrelated."

As the funeral director looked on, Geoff began a close study of the upper legs, working toward the ankles. I cleaned my own magnifier with a paper towel from an embalming table dispenser and zeroed in on the head burns.

"The point of impact," I commented as I worked, "is exactly where Throckingham said it was. If Strong was standing straight . . . yes, the burn pattern's circular. If Strong was standing, then the ray or bolt or whatever it was couldn't have come from anything as low down as the trees. It had to come from almost directly overhead. And if it emanated from the library roof, one would expect impact on the back of the skull, not just above the forehead." I began scrutinizing the face and neck. "There also appear to be minute surface burns following several pathways downward."

"Yes," Weston commented, "I see the trickle marks running down the legs, too. Surely a laser strike wouldn't produce that pattern. Burning would be more localized and deeper."

I sighed and shifted my attention to the torso.

"True but discouraging. What are we left with but lightning? The pattern's definitely electrical. It's consistent with a lightning strike. But the Tazer gun's the only device I know that can accurately guide an electrical charge, and there certainly aren't any puncture marks to show wired electrodes have been shot into him."

"Besides," Geoff took up the commentary, "not even a souped up Tazer could produce this pattern, and it certainly wouldn't, if Throckingham's telling the truth, jolt a bystander off his feet."

I shifted the corpse to its side and examined the back.

"Negative on the scars," I concluded. "The only operation he ever underwent was to remove his wisdom teeth. No puncture marks . . . plenty of bruises though. He must have jerked into the air from muscle contractions, then fallen hard. The body evidence here seems quite plain. Lightning struck the head, traveled down the skin surface, and, while he was still in a standing position, arced to ground from his feet. It's as simple as that."

"You're probably right," Geoff agreed grudgingly. By now his glass hovered over the bottom of the victim's foot. "I can even make out burns where electricity jumped the gap from his heel to the cobbler's nails. My, that nail pattern is a might unusual. I'll want a picture of it for the record. You might also shoot the head and a close-up of the torso surface burns. Take Polaroids for quick reference and some negative shots we can blow up later."

He straightened up and turned toward the mortician. "Mr. . . . ."

"Stout. Robert Stout."

"Bob, we'll need to have a look at the victim's personal effects."

Our host nodded and gestured with his thumb toward the side wall. "They're in one of the lockers."

He withdrew a key from his trouser pocket and accompanied Geoff in that direction while I pulled cameras and lenses from my photo bag and got down to work. A few seconds later I heard a locker open and glanced briefly across the room. Geoff had donned white gloves and was digging into the piled up contents.

"The deceased's wallet and jewelry," Stout announced stiffly, "have been returned to the widow. She has not, however, provided us with a burial suit, so what you have there are the clothes he was wearing when the hospital transferred the remains to us."

I began snapping close-ups of both feet. Geoff was right. The nail patterns were so far toward the edge of the heels that at times the arcing came from beyond the ball perimeter entirely. I turned toward my partner to offer a comment, but thought better of it since he seemed engrossed in studying the shoes. I switched to the Polaroid to take back-up shots which we'd have the mortician sign for possible courtroom use.

At length Weston looked up from his examination.

"These shoes," he pronounced, "aren't the ones Senator

Strong had on when he died."

The mortician reacted with unbelievably suave skepticism.

"Of course they are. You can see the burn marks yourself and mud splattered on the uppers. It was raining, you know, on the day he died. I bet if we try the shoes on him, they'll fit like they were made for him."

"I'm sure they will," my partner acknowledged. "The thief was far too clever for such a crude mistake. But he made his share of blunders along the way." Geoff held a shoe up under Stout's aqualine nose. "You'll notice, for instance, that these have never been waxed. They're completely new except for having been torched on the bottom. Even there the charring isn't more pronounced around the heel tacks as it should be." He turned the footwear so Bob's eyes stared down its throat. "You'll notice that *these* shoes have never even been worn. Socks haven't polished the high spots on the interior leather. And, miracle of miracles, electricity arced off his burned feet, passed through the cobbler nails and burned the heels *without* doing any damage to the leather pad that shields his feet from the brads." He rotated the shoe again to display the heel. "What's more, the nail pattern isn't even close to matching the scars on the Senator's feet. Where, Mr. Stout, are the right shoes?"

"I . . . I . . . " Bob seemed shaken by the onslaught. "I don't know. But I assure you none of our staff . . . I mean . . . the shoes must have been switched at the hospital. Our reputation is impeccable, impeccable, and we can't afford even a suggestion of scandal."

As Weston slid the shoes into a plastic bag, I shot my last picture and stepped over to join the action.

"Please sign and date these photos," I instructed him. "We may need you to testify when they're entered into evidence."

"Testify?" Stout's fingers automatically closed on the stack. "But that's impossible. The firm can't . . . . "

"Meanwhile," I volunteered, "Geoff and I will search the premises for signs of forced entry. We aren't making

50

accusations, and we jolly well want to do whatever we can to clear you."

"*Clear* me? I haven't done anything."

"I doubt that you have," Weston joined in, "but for your reputation's sake you must want us to prove it."

"Yes, of course, but ... "

Geoff held the locker padlock under his lens and scrutinized its keyhole.

"Does this place have electronic security?"

"Are you kidding? What's to steal in a mortuary?"

"Shoes," I responded. "Do you mind if I examine the lock to the service entrance?"

The funeral director shrugged in defeat. "Do whatever you must."

"Thanks. Please sign each snapshot on the back just under my initials."

I left the perspiring mortician fumbling in his breast pocket for a pen and strolled over to the basement's steel outside door. It was probably far too late to get meaningful prints in the unlikely event some intruder hadn't worn gloves, but I turned the knob carefully with two fingers wrapped in a paper towel. The outside was, of course, an impossibility since rain was still sheeting down the stairwell and had drenched everything. I knelt down and peered at the drop-spattered lockset.

"The pick marks," I reported aloud, "are quite distinct. Our burglar was most probably in a hurry."

"Aren't they usually," Weston noted. "This padlock is scratched up a might also." He plopped it into a bag matter-of-factly and then put his arm around our host's shoulders. "It looks as though the firm's out of the woods. You'd better phone the police and report the break-in though. Be sure to mention that the shoes were custom-made. That elevates the matter to grand theft and should assure us a more vigorous investigation."

"And just why," Stout asked miserably, "do we want a vigorous investigation?"

"Because," my partner responded, "the body doesn't get buried until the matter's resolved."

We accompanied the funeral director to his office and satisfied ourselves that he did report the crime. In fact, he'd hardly hung up the telephone when a police cruiser pulled up out front and two bored officers approached the mortuary. Headquarters, it turned out, was only two blocks distant. Unfortunately, the men seemed nearly as bored after we passed on the facts of the case to them as before. They did, however, agree to brush the doorknob, shoes and lock for fingerprints. I had a feeling they viewed the situation as slightly bizarre but generally on a par with bicycle theft. We had to literally force them to impound the padlock and shoes as evidence.

By the time we left the building the rain had decreased to a misty drizzle. I must admit that my own mood was a might drizzily, too, as we continued walking up Wisconsin Avenue toward Bradley Lane. I hadn't at all expected that kind of official reaction. My partner, however, didn't seem unduly concerned. As we hiked by the telephone company office, though, he paused to make some calls from the public booth. When he emerged a few moments later, he was all smiles.

"You look," I noted curiously, "like the cat who swallowed the canary. I expect you to break into whistling any minute."

Weston practiced a couple of puckers. "Now that you've made the suggestion," he assured me, "any psychologist will tell you it's practically assured. Old bean, I thought we could get the ball rolling by cajoling the undertaker to our side. That didn't produce the results we wanted, but I now *guarantee* swift action."

"Who'd you call?" I demanded with some trepidation.

He savored the tidbit for an infuriating ten seconds.

"How do headlines like KILLER SHOES STOLEN FROM SENATOR'S BODY or MYSTERIOUS MORTUARY SWITCH strike you? *Post* and *Times* reporters will be

"That," Geoff acknowledged, "would seem to be the case. Your phone was tapped, you know. We're now convinced the murderer blew that Concorde out of the sky because he thought we'd be on it. So we're also dealing with mass murder. John and I aren't quite certain yet how your husband was killed, but it seems that his shoes were somehow involved. Would he perhaps have a similar pair we could examine?"

She stomped her foot. "Ooh, I should have known better. You're going to hate me."

"Let me guess," Weston responded. "Someone came up the street shouting 'New lamps for old.' "

She scowled and shook her head in frustration. "It was just about that bad. A man called from a charity I support and offered me his sympathies. Then he suggested I avoid the pain of being reminded about Jim every time I opened the closet. He said he'd send a truck for my donations and he did. I was so stupid! I even let the driver pick out the clothes he'd leave behind for the funeral. I should have realized Good Will wouldn't solicit from widows. But it seemed so natural!"

"Most confidence schemes do," my partner acknowledged. "Don't blame yourself. I probably would have done the same thing in your place."

I switched off the frequency scanner.

"Could you," I inquired, "give us a description of the driver. That might help."

She stared into space as though trying to visualize the man.

"Well, he was dressed in olive drab coveralls with a phoney charity emblem on front, although of course I didn't know that then. He was blond, maybe twenty-five, average height, and looked muscular. Let's see . . . he had kind of a rounded face and a barrel chest. I've seen army sergeants on television that looked just like him."

"And did he," I persisted, "have a small scar on his chin?"

"Why yes, I believe he did. How did you know that?"

"Because he was one of the two chaps who just tried to end

59

our careers. It's just as well you were taken in by him or he might have used more desperate means to get what he wanted."

"Oh dear. What have I gotten you into?"

"Into a most challenging investigation," Weston assured her. "We wouldn't have missed it for the world. We will, however, need a bit of help from you."

"Anything."

"Do you think you could convince your husband's staff to work on some projects for us?"

She hesitated. "You know, of course, that I don't have any authority, and the staff itself is just tying up loose ends until the governor can appoint someone to . . . . "

"I realize all that," Geoff replied. "I'm not talking about official authority or normal channels. Appeal to their loyalty. Will they make some unofficial studies for you?"

"I . . . I think so. What information do you need?"

"I need," my partner rattled off, "a computer readout comparing Senator Strong's and Senator Kidd's voting records over the last year as well as their projected votes on pending legislation. I need copies of their speeches both on and off the Senate floor. I need lists of special interest groups they either backed or offended or both. I want to know all the personal and political bridges your husband was building in preparation for a presidential bid, and every toe on which he stepped. I'd also like Mrs. Kidd's telephone number."

She had pulled a notebook from her dress pocket and was writing down the requests.

"I think I can get all that for you. And as for Phyllis's number, I'll just jot that down for you right now. We play tennis together, you know, so we keep in touch." She turned a page in her notebook and began scribbling the information.

"We'll also want," Geoff continued, "any Library of Congress books your husband may still have on loan. The volumes downtown at the office have no doubt been returned, but if he brought anything home with him . . . . "

"I believe," she considered aloud, "there is one on the

nightstand." She tore out the sheet of paper and handed it briskly to Weston. "Why don't we all go in and I'll get it for you. You two are going to catch your death standing out here in those wet clothes. Would you like some tea?"

"Why, thank you," I responded appreciatively. "That *would* hit the spot." We began moving toward the porch. "You wouldn't have any idea, would you, where and when your husband bought his shoes or had them repaired?"

She mulled the matter over as we strolled up the drive.

"Oh, it's been at least several months on either count. We have a shoemaker friend back home in California who does all our repair work for us, so we save it up while the Senate's in session. I seem to remember, though .... What was the name? Capitol Hill Footwear .... Capitol Hill Custom Shoes .... Something like that. Anyway, they were just getting started in the neighborhood and sent Jim's office a flyer a little after New Year's offering both mass produced and handmade shoes at special introductory prices. Mr. Taylor, do you know how much walking politicians do? Jim was tickled at the idea of buying some really reasonable custom-made shoes to see if they made a difference. As I remember, a man even came to the office to take a cast of his foot, so it wasn't any bother at all."

"And how were they picked up?" Weston interposed.

"Why, Jim went to the shop personally to try on both pairs and make sure they fit. He told me they were just perfect. The company even threw in a couple of gold-plated shoe horns with their name and address engraved on them. I believe I've still got one lying around somewhere. Do you want me to find it for you?"

"That, madam," Geoff responded, "isn't a question. It's an understatement!"

Just as Mrs. Strong escorted us inside, I heard a momentary siren blast and turned to see a police sedan slow as it passed by out front. My first reaction was to wonder how they'd responded so quickly to the 'accident' when all the phones were dead. My second was to wonder if it was a *real* police cruiser. I closed the door behind me, took out my electronic snooper, and methodically tested the house for bugs. There were none.

A few moments later Geoff and I were seated at a cherrywood dining table sipping tea as electric heaters warmed our feet and a chandelier sparkled overhead. Across the table Mrs. Strong gazed at us over the rim of her cup.

"You know, it really hasn't sunk in that Jim's dead yet. We've been together for so many years that I still catch myself expecting him to come home at the usual hour. I go to sleep at night and dream he's standing there talking about the future with that boundless enthusiasm of his." A tear trickled down her cheek and she wiped it away hastily.

"Then I wake up, and I'm so unspeakably angry. I'm angry with the whole world for continuing normally, with those animals who killed him, and even with God for letting it happen. Then I'm even madder at myself for reacting that way. Jim and I had good years together and I should be able to let go—knowing he's with Jesus . . . but it's so *hard.*" She paused to sip her tea. "I keep pushing myself to stay so busy there's no time to think. When I finally do slow down, I'll begin to be lonely and then Jim's death will be real to me. When that happens, I don't want to still be carrying around questions. I want someone in jail. I want . . . not vengeance . . . *justice.* If only we'd had children, it wouldn't be so lonely. If only God hadn't let Jim die!"

Geoff gazed into her eyes with deep concern.

"Frankly," he confessed, "I don't have anything to say that won't seem like putting a bandaid on an amputated limb. I want you to know, though, that I can and do share your sorrow. I'm not just mouthing a cliche when I say I know how you feel." Weston took a sip from his own cup.

"When I was growing up, I was one of those chaps who actually fell in love with the girl next door. That happens now and then, you know. I'd play jacks with her. She'd play

62

football, that's soccer in America, with me. Neither of us doubted for a moment that we'd someday be married. She was quite a wonderful girl, actually, and over the years she developed into a sensitive, caring, vivacious, beautiful young woman. Too beautiful.... She was kidnapped just after school one day at the age of fifteen."

He paused to collect his thoughts. "It's my only unsolved case. I was too young then to know what to do, and by the time I became a detective, too much time had gone by. People's memories had faded. Clues had vanished. Sometimes I wonder what she's thinking... if she's alive. When I first heard the gospel, I actually resisted because she wasn't there to respond with me. It didn't seem fair. It still doesn't, but looking back I can recognize a few of the reasons God may have had in allowing the tragedy. Every solved case is a reason because I doubt I'd have taken up my profession but for what happened to her. Every crime averted... every life saved... in the balances of logic it's a good trade. Sometimes, however, we human beings are very illogical. That's our great weakness, as well as our strength. We simply have to trust and love God amidst grief. That's the lesson of Job. 'Though he slay me, yet will I praise him.' God sees the big picture. We see a part. We pray for His will—while usually meaning ours. He sifts through the thousands of sometimes conflicting prayers, knowing who needs what and who gets what and how what one person gets affects the future needs of others. He works all things together for good for His children, but 'good' doesn't mean 'painlessness.' "

This time when a tear trickled down Mrs. Strong's cheek she didn't brush it away.

"But how can you be sure," she questioned, "that it all works for the good? There's so *much* pain."

"In the garden," Geoff responded, "Satan put that same proposition to history's only perfect woman. She couldn't handle it intellectually even with a flawless brain. Don't think you'll do any better. We're living on a flyspeck planet in endless space using limited intelligence to sift woefully incomplete data. None of us has any chance of logically proving God's purposes or absolute promises. We'd have to be God. We aren't, so you and I are literally forced to depend on and accept what our mind's inventor tells us about Himself. The alternative is despair. Don't distrust Him or you'll regret it."

"You sound," Cathleen Strong observed, "as though you've walked down that road yourself."

Geoff smiled ruefully. "Yes, I've hiked down that trail. Before becoming a Christian I read the Bible avidly and satisfied myself that its fulfilled prophecies proved absolutely it was God's Word. I could prove God's power and design from a look at the universe and the lack of a viable, scientific alternative to creation. The testimony and changed lives of the apostles seemed legally acceptable and compelling evidence for Christ's resurrection. But try as I might, I couldn't prove God's character. Oh, I could see consistent demonstrations to man of His righteousness, generosity, love, etc., but I fell short of absolute proof since mankind's experience itself was limited and earthbound.

"I beat my head against a brick wall for several months until I finally realized Satan's wicked wisdom in tempting Eve with the only lie human logic couldn't disprove. Was it Tertullian who said, 'I believe because it is absurd'? I wouldn't go that far, but I concluded that logic only carries one so far and no further. Beyond that point only faith can travel. Logic can't fathom the Infinite, but faith can accept Him on the basis of what He reveals of Himself. I placed my personal trust in Christ and haven't been disappointed. Don't you be either. God the Father gave His own Son to die for you and Jim. Don't rebel against Him now for considering you worthy to suffer a little—to have your faith strengthened by testing. As for John's and my part, we'll do all we can to see that justice is done and that you don't have to carry around the added emotional baggage of wondering who committed the murder or why."

Up to that time I had been content to remain a bystander, munching bakery cookies, sipping an excellent blend of black teas, and listening to what was to me a startling conversation. During Geoff's sympathetic response to our client, he had revealed more about himself than he'd told me in all our years of association. Now, at last, I thought I understood his reluctance to endanger women by dating them. Paloma was the exception and I rather wondered why.

"Mrs. Strong," I declared with hopes of steering the talk back to less personal aspects of the case, "what's your impression of Senator Throckingham?"

She took a cookie and set it on her saucer's edge.

"Oh, I guess you'd call him a dear, lovable rogue. He's so openly calculating that you wonder if he really means it. I find myself liking him even when I despise everything he says."

"Does he," I pursued the matter, "have any hope of being nominated for the presidency?"

"No. None at all."

Geoff balanced the book that Mrs. Strong had given us spine down on the table and let it fall open of its own accord.

"Do you have any idea," he asked, "why your husband was reading a book on psychotic diseases?" He looked down at the chapter heading. "More specifically, a chapter on schizophrenia and multiple personalties?"

"No," she responded, "I don't. There may have been some mental health legislation coming up soon, but I can't recall any."

"He wasn't, perhaps, trying to diagnose some individual?"

Mrs. Strong sipped her tea while she considered the possibility.

"He could have been checking on someone he'd heard about. Constituents were always asking favors. Someone might have approached Jim about finding treatment for a family member. He's helped a few veterans into V.A. hospitals."

"I see," Weston said, closing the book. "Would you make an inquiry for us with the staff about that?"

"Certainly." She wrote an additional reminder in her notebook. "Shouldn't you report that attempt on your lives while the police are still outside?"

"That would be the logical thing to do," Weston replied. "Therefore, we won't do it either here or at the precinct headquarters. Someone's doing a good job of anticipating our moves and I mean to put a stop to it. You, however, should report both the phone tap and attempted murder to both the locals, the FBI, and the Secret Service. Use a pay phone." He took the two transmitters from his shirt pocket and handed them across to her. "See that only the FBI gets these. Call them first. Wire tapping's in their jurisdiction and the locals seem a might apathetic anyway. Insist that the Secret Service provide bodyguards. Does your automobile have a burglar alarm?"

"Yes, it does."

"Use it. Balance toothpicks in door jams and just under the hood whenever you leave it. Check them when you return and don't even touch the vehicle if they've been dislodged. Even if they're still there, check under the car for both bombs and cut brake lines before entering."

Cathleen smiled. "That is going to play havoc with my evening dresses. You think, then, that they'll attack me?

"They might, but probably not before I force them into the open. Up until now their attempts to murder us have been disguised as terrorism and drunk driving to avoid prompting a more thorough investigation of your husband's death. By morning, though, I'm going to blow the lid off. Then you may be in danger. Do you have a gun?"

"Several. My husband was a member of the National Rifle Association. We went target shooting together. As a matter of fact, I have extras if you'd care for some. I know you couldn't bring any on the plane."

"We would, indeed," I noted regretfully, "but unfortunately we lack an American license."

"License schmicense." She seemed indignant. "I'm talking rifles and shotguns, not pistols. You don't need one unless you carry them around town in an unlocked container. Lock them in your car trunk. Store them in your hotel room. This is America, not Europe."

Weston barely suppressed a smile. "You forget, madam, that we're somewhat lacking in both automobile and boot . . . ah, trunk . . . at the moment. However, we appreciate your offer. If that is, indeed, the law then . . . "

"Use mine," she interrupted. "I have two. Now that Jim's gone, I only need one."

"But," I protested, "it might get blown up or rammed. We can't guarantee . . . . "

She stared at me across the table. "I'm insured, Mr. Taylor, and I won't have either of you killed on my account."

"Are you," Weston inquired, "in the habit of loaning out your vehicles to acquaintances?"

"No, never. But this is an exception."

"Very good," my partner remarked. "We'll accept it."

6
SUBMARINE ALLEY

Traffic was heavy on Connecticut Avenue. Fortunately, however, most of it was headed out of town. We were making good time. To our right, a block-long office building covered with mirrors jutted high overhead, its circular corner stairwells looking for all the world like engine pods. I half expected the whole thing to rocket into the sky.

"Wall, Pard," I attempted in my best Texas accent, "how does it feel ta be in the rootin' tootin' shootin' east part of the West with rifles in our boot and sittin' in a Cadillac?"

Geoff changed lanes to avoid a lorry parked illegally by the curb.

"It feels," he commented with a chuckle, "as though we're missing one important ingredient."

"What's that?"

"The steer horn on our bonnet."

"But that," I pointed out reproachfully, "might make usn' just a leedle bit conspicuous."

Weston rolled his eyes. "What do you think we are now with senatorial license plates?" He changed the subject. "Have you found anything of use in those pictures yet?"

"A might. Enlargements would tell us more, but you can hardly expect that kind of service from a one-hour photomat. We did well to get what we got, and I for one am rather glad we had extras to mail to the FBI. The more they know, the less reason the killer has to dispose of us."

"Or try to," Geoff agreed. "What about the pictures?"

I shuffled through the stack and aimed my magnifying lens at one of the most promising.

"The driver of the pick-up," I observed, "was wearing a

stocking mask over his head, so we're not going to get an identification there." I studied another shot then rejected it. "When the lorry hit that bush it kicked up so much mud and leaves I don't have a clear view of the rear bumper. There does seem, however, to be some sort of green sticker on it. It could be a parking permit for a school or some government agency. I can't, though, read it. That, I'm afraid, will take computer enhancement if it's readable at all."

"And the license plate?"

"I'll try for that from a view of the front. Ah, here it is. It's Maryland plate number HJB-741. You know as well as I do, though, that both the plate and the pick-up are almost certainly stolen. By now they're either at the bottom of the Potomac or ground to nuggets in a junk yard."

Weston gunned the engine and accelerated through an intersection before the yellow light turned red.

"You're probably right about that," he admitted, "but I'm glad we've got the photos. There are occasionally witnesses to auto thefts or dumpings. The more individual crimes we uncover, the better chance we'll develop a lead and at last identify some underling."

"Who," I added, "was probably hired for a single job and knows nothing beyond that."

Geoff ignored my pessimism. "What about the shots on the Mazda and the assassin?"

"Clear, sharp, and detailed. We have a license number and a picture of the chap's face that should almost guarantee a mug book identification if he's got a record."

"That's something," Geoff declared with satisfaction. "The lad must be on the payroll rather than a mere contract worker or he wouldn't be popping up collecting for charities."

Weston one-handed the wheel while he groped for the radio telephone. In the interest of safety I reached out and beat him to it.

"I'll dial for you," I offered. "Do you think it's wise, though, to broadcast our moves?"

"Probably not," he passed me the slip of paper with the number. "But I'll take the chance we have a few moments at least before our 'chess player' catches on. The investigation's got to accelerate or we're in trouble. Either we act so fast all he can do is react, or we just may wake up dead tomorrow."

I pressed buttons, then handed him the phone as the ringing on the line halted with a click.

"Hallo. I'd like to speak with Mrs. Kidd, please.... You are? Mrs. Kidd, this is Geoffrey Weston of Sleuth's Ltd. Cathleen Strong has retained us to investigate her.... Oh, you've heard. Well, would you mind answering a few questions?"

Geoff maneuvered the auto around a pick-up that had stalled at a stop light.

"First I'd like to know if your husband ever bought shoes from an establishment known as Capitol Hill Custom Shoes?... In mid-January, I see. A single pair? Was he wearing them at the time of the accident?... I'd surmised as much. Other than the Mexican arms package, can you think of any pending legislation that both your husband and Senator Strong could have influenced decisively in either direction?... You can't. Well, thank you ever so much for your time. If you think of anything that might help, please pass it on to Mrs. Strong and she'll let us know.... It was a pleasure at this end, too. Ta ta."

Weston handed me the phone as we sped past the National Zoo and an entrance to canyon-like Rock Creek Park. He didn't so much as glance in their direction.

"See if you can raise Blair House. We're going to have a chat with President Guerrero."

"And his daughter?"

"Possibly."

I studied his face for a reaction but didn't catch so much as a flicker. Either he was hiding his feelings well, or he was intensely preoccupied with the mystery. I rather suspected it was a little of both. I dutifully dialed information, jotted down the stilted, computer-generated numbers that came in response to my query, and touch-toned the sequence. My reward was a flat, man's voice.

"The Blair House. May I help you?"

"Quite possibly," I informed him. "This is John Taylor and Geoffrey Weston. We're personal friends of Augustin and Paloma Guerrero. I assume they're staying at Blair House during their state visit. Would it be possible to have a word with either of them?"

"Please hold the line while I see if they're in."

Before I could reply, there was a click and background music floated tinnily into my ear. While waiting I gazed down from the bridge we were motoring across at meandering, boulder-strewn Rock Creek and a forest held at bay by grassy meadows bordering an asphalt parkway. The phone clicked again.

"*Ay que,* Geoffrey!" I recognized the young lady's melodic Spanish. "It's so very good to hear from you again. I have a thousand questions, *mil preguntas y . . .* "

"You'd be asking the wrong person," I interrupted. "This is John. Wait a minute and I'll put Geoff on the phone." I extended the receiver toward him. "It's Paloma."

He seemed to relax into the seat as he took the receiver.

"*Como estas, Palomita*? . . . No. I'm not calling from London. We're in Washington . . . Yes. Really . . . . Of course we'll get together. What about your father? Could he. . . .I see . . . . No, I certainly wouldn't want to throw him off schedule. I realize there are hundreds of Congressmen and a hundred Senators. Boy, do I realize it! We'll be visiting some of them ourselves. Do you think your papa would accept John as a suitable chaparone if we went to dinner together? . . . A Secret Service escort, too? Is that necessary? I see . . . No, I didn't read about it. I'm afraid *Time* is more partial to European and American news. If they ran that story at all, they buried it. Was anybody hurt? . . . Is he expected to recover? . . . That's good. I'll be praying for him. What time shall we come by? . . . No, we can't right now. We're headed somewhere on business . . . . All right, eight-thirty, but isn't that a little late to eat? . . . Ah, then this must be your first day here . . . . Yes, the time zone hopping has affected us, too . . . . Your guess is correct. We are on a case . . . . I'm afraid I can't say anything over the phone. We'll talk about it tonight. *Hasta luego. Y que Dios te bendiga.*"

Geoff recradled the phone and swung the Cadillac into the outer lane of Dupont Circle.

"If the glove compartment map's correct," he commented, "this is where we change over to Massachusetts Avenue heading east. Keep an eye peeled for it."

I started craning my neck to make out signs.

"Done. There's . . . no, that's headed west. I'm amazed," I added tongue-in-cheek, "at the relentless interrogation you gave Paloma. What's this Palom*ita*, anyway? Does it mean little dove, little pigeon, or popcorn? Ah, there's Massachusetts. Take a quick right." Wheels squealed as my partner followed my directions quite literally.

I glanced over at Geoff and noticed with chagrin that his face from the neck up looked as though it had been dipped into a vat of red dye. I'd seldom seen such an obvious blush. He was evidently a good deal more sensitive about the girl than I'd suspected. To make amends for my bantering, I ignored his appearance and continued in a more serious vein.

"What's this about someone being injured? Were they in an accident?"

"No," Weston responded grimly. "Someone sprayed Paloma's limosine with gunfire last week. The driver was badly wounded but managed to keep the auto going and get her to safety. She thinks they thought her father was inside. Add another act of terrorism to our growing list."

A few minutes later, our Cadillac turned onto Pennsylvania Avenue where it forked off from Independence near the Library of Congress. Row on row of shops fitted with accordion-like burglar bars spoke openly of violence or the fear of it. As we were forced to a more leisurely pace by the vehicles in front, I studied the shops looking for the 417

72

address that was engraved in a certain gold plated shoe horn. There was an Italian restaurant, a barber shop, a dry cleaners . . . I almost missed it.

"Turn down the next side street," I commanded. "We've gone past. You're not going to like this. It's not a shoe store anymore. Our shoemaker's taken a hike."

We parked just around the corner and retraced our steps to a quaint shop whose show windows fairly dripped hanging sausages, cheeses, and strings of pungent garlic. The sign over the green and white striped awning declared that we were approaching "The New York Deli." We followed the aroma of roast beef and freshly baked bread through the entrance and found ourselves confronting a refrigerated glass counter filled with scrumptious looking dainties. Behind the case a balding, pot-bellied gent in a white apron was in animated conversation with a customer. While I waited in line, Geoff paced around the area open to the public, sniffing salamies and looking for dust in the corners. Twice he bent down and picked up a speck. Fortunately, the proprietor was having such a good time he didn't notice.

" . . . and so I has this flat while driving the Cross Bronx Expressway, see." He waved a loaf of French bread for emphasis. "And I paks da ca' and jacks up da back end. And I'm takin' off da tire when dis guy pulls up behind me. I looks up and sees he's jackin' up da otha' side. So I yells out 'Hey, buddy, wudaya think yer doin'? So he sez, 'Don't be greedy. You take dat side and I'll take dis'. So I yells, 'Get oudda hea', you scuz; it's my ca'!" The proprietor slapped his side with his free hand and boomed forth with an infectious belly laugh. "New Yo'k! Der's no place like it. Mr. Liebowitz, ya godda go der sometime." He handed a bag across the counter. "Yer momma's gonna love these Kosher hoagies. If she don't, you let me know, okay? I'll give ya yer money back. See ya next week."

He looked my way, the broad smile on his face putting his bulbous nose into almost normal proportions.

"May I help youse gentlemen?"

I peered at the prices on the wall behind him.

"Well," I ventured, "we might go with a couple of your Submarine Supremes."

He slapped the counter. "I knew it when I first seen ya. Ya got culture."

The proprietor selected several cheeses and meats from the refrigerator and began shaving off mounds of paper-thin slices with a rotary slicer.

"Da thinna' da pieces," he informed me, "da more flava' gets released."

"You sound," I volunteered, "as though you've got a lot of experience. Have you been here long?"

"Naw. Only about a month. And I wouldn'ta had da chance den, but some bird welched on his lease. Lucky fer me. It's a good location. Skully moved out, see, and two weeks lata' here I was. Business has been growin' eva' since. Already I gotta regula' clientel."

"That wouldn't be James Skully, would it?"

"Don't think so. I believe it said 'Nate' on da sign." He waved a Polish dill back and forth over the slicer. "I'll say dis fer da guy. He sure left da place clean. My carpentas didn't even havta tear out old displays. Dat's how I got in so quick." He split a French roll lengthwise with a butcher knife, spread on a dark mustard, and began layering the meat and cheese, topping them with pickle, lettuce and other accouterments. "Der's an art ta makin' a good sub. Add too much mustard, ya ovapowa yer cheese. Add too little, and it's dry. Ya know what I mean?"

"I certainly do," I assured him. "It's amazing how one little condiment can make all the difference." I reached in my wallet for the appropriate bills. "I notice it's the same way with people's lives, too. One little decision can spell the difference between success and failure, even between heaven and hell." I placed the bill on the counter and laid a gospel booklet down beside it.

He closed the buns and skewered them with toothpicks.

"Now yer talkin' like a preacha. Don't take no offense if ya are, now. It's a fine profession."

"I sound," I corrected him, "even more like someone saying what some preachers say to say."

The proprietor wrapped the two submarines, slipped them into a bag and deposited the lot on the counter in front of me.

"Ya do fer a fact," he agreed as he pocketed the tract and started ringing up the bill. "I'm always jumpin' to conclusions."

"I don't mind being mistaken for a man of the cloth," I assured him, "except that some people assume my real motive is acquiring church members. Read the booklet when you get a chance, and you'll see that's not it at all."

"Sure." He punched the total button on the register and started making change from the cash drawer. "Da next time youse two come in, I'll gives ya a repo't."

I smiled as I held out my hand for the coins.

"Now who's acting like a professional?" I kidded him. "Isn't the cardinal rule of vending 'Promise anything to keep the customer coming back'?"

"Naw," he responded. "I really mean it. I'll ... "

Weston strode over from near the hanging sausages. "Gentlemen, I hate to interrupt this delightful chat, but we are running somewhat late for an appointment. Sir," he addressed the New Yorker, "I would like to get in touch with that shoemaker if at all possible. He has some shoes I'd very much like to look at. Could you give us the name of the real estate firm from which you rent? They may have a forwarding address on this Mr. Skully."

"It's da Rawlin's Agency."

"The Rawlings Agency," Weston scribbled the information down in his pad. "They're probably closed by now, but perhaps we can ring them in the morning. Good day Mr. ... "

"Blanda. Mike Blanda. Jus' call me Mike."

"Good evening Mr. .... Mike. Rest assured we will be back for that report. Incidentally, I'm not a preacher either."

Blanda eyed my partner up and down from his goatee and disheveled hair to his mud-stained sneakers.

"Somehow," he observed, "I figgered ya wasn't." He snapped his fingers as if struck by a sudden thought. "Next time why don't ya try a hot pastrami. I make one ya godda taste ta believe. I'll even give ya a discount. Like I says, I want regula' customas."

I picked up the bag and pocketed my change. "We'll keep that in mind," I promised.

Geoff and I strode from the delicatessen and headed toward our automobile at the end of the block. As it turned out, however, we walked right by the auto, pausing only to drop off the submarines, and turned down the alley to search the area behind the deli. We were none too soon, and I could see why my partner had cut our visit with the store owner short. Shadows were lengthening and the western sky had reddened signalling twilight's approach. It wouldn't be an easy job to search thoroughly in the time remaining.

"You take the area around the dust bin," Weston whispered. "The can's new, so there's no need to look inside, but check underneath. Even if they swept up, they may have forgotten that spot."

"Righto." I descended to my hands and knees, extracted my glass from my coat and started examining the asphalt pavement square by imaginary square. Meanwhile Geoff walked a few yards down the alley and peered into what must have been the shop owner's Ford LTD, an old petrol-guzzling dinosaur that still sported New York plates. I returned to my own investigation and had soon bagged an assortment of thoroughly uninteresting sundries. Pieces of orange peel, beer-can tabs, and chunks of wax cheese coating were hardly my idea of prime clues. I lifted the ash bin to set it aside and . . . .

"Hallo," I whispered under my breath. "What have we here?" A slight depression in the asphalt had filled with silt from muddy runoffs. The afternoon shower had caused enough seepage to re-wet the area and expose just the corner of some sort of card. I worked my pocket knife blade under the paper and lifted gently until my find was freed from its encasing sediment. Then it was just a matter of bathing the card ever so carefully in the puddle. As the mud slowly washed away, the first words that became decipherable were "Stacks pass" and "Library of Congress." The pre-printed portions were still fairly legible, but the typed-in blanks had all but washed out and the lines reserved for issuer and recipient's signatures were a mere blue haze. They'd evidently been filled in with water soluble ink. I mounted the card on my notebook's plastic cover to dry and continued stirring the waters of mini Loch Ness with my finger. Fortunately it was a job depending on sense of touch rather than sight, because the alleyway was becoming decidedly dim. I noticed Geoff crawling around beside and even partway under the motorcar and marvelled at how infrequently he resorted to his mini torch. I added a few curled shavings of what I took to be neolite to my collection and finally bagged everything in plastic—including my notebook—and struggled resignedly back to my feet. My knees were dented, my legs were cramped, and I was most definitely ready for a hot shower and a deli sandwich. Weston, when he emerged from under the Ford's engine, looked even readier than I. The car evidently suffered from an oil leak. I helped him up and handed him a handkerchief to wipe his blackened palms and ear.

"I would suggest," I spoke in low tones, "that we get out of here before Mr. Blanda closes shop or empties the garbage."

"I think you're right," Geoff agreed. "We'd better go while there's still enough power in my torch so we can check the Cadillac for tampering."

"You," I corrected him. "So *you* can crawl underneath. The chassis's so low I won't fit ... fortunately. Besides, you're already dressed for it."

Geoff ignored my comment as we retraced our steps up the alley. "When we get home," he thought aloud, "it shouldn't take you long to test the sandwiches for poison."

I blinked at that since there were literally thousands of tests for specific toxins. Then I visualized myself drooling over Blanda's masterpieces while dissecting and analyzing them.

"You are developing," I concluded with considerable feeling, "a full-blown case of paranoia."

My fear of an all-night vigil proved groundless, however. On the way home, Geoff detoured to a pet store we'd passed earlier and which, for some peculiar reason, was still open. He'd settled on a most simple and effective test for food adulteration. A white rat, it seemed, was going to eat our dinner. Oh well, I consoled myself, there was still the dinner date with Paloma, although it would have been nice to squeeze three meals into the day even at outrageous hours.

7
A WITNESS TO MURDER

It's amazing what a steamy, tingling shower can do to soothe away exhaustion. Dry, warm, unwrinkled clothes also have a certain therapeutic effect. A cup of tea on top of that warms the insides and produces an almost complete cure. I was actually enjoying my second cup of tea and managing to ignore the long-nosed rodent munching happily away in its corner cage. The "ignoring" was aided, of course, by an assemblage of possible clues strewn before me on the kitchen table and demanding attention. I squeezed a drop of chemicals from an eyedropper onto the still damp stacks pass and studied the spot under my lens.

"We are getting a reaction with trace amounts of ink," I declared in a loud voice. "A little of the typing's re-appearing."

Weston's voice boomed from the bathroom where he was dressing. "Good. Can you make out to whom the pass was issued?"

I carefully squeezed a couple of additional drops onto the pertinent blank.

"It seems to be ... " I leaned forward in my chair and strained to make out the faint, fuzzy letters. "It starts with a T - U - L ... No, that first letter's probably a J. There's room for two more letters in the first name, but I can't raise them. The last name starts with R $blank$ DR and the rest is missing."

"JUL blank blank." Geoff echoed. "That could be Julia, Julie, Jules or Julio. R blank DR surely has to be Rodriguez. I can't think of anything else with that combination, can you?"

"There's always Roderick," I pointed out, "if we suppose the typist didn't know how to spell. But since that Mexican aid vote may tie in with this mess somewhere, Rodriguez sounds like a likely choice."

"You don't know the half of it," Weston responded. "I found a genuine, minted-in-Mexico *veinte* under Blanda's motorcar. It must have fallen out of some driver's pocket when he fished for his keys. Later, someone swept around an automobile then parked there but neglected to consider that something might have rolled underneath."

"Then," I concluded, "there had to be two people involved in the shoe affair—Rodriguez and that chap Skully."

The bathroom door was flung open and Geoff stepped forth in all his sartorial splendor. I'd never actually seen him in a black bow tie, ruffled shirt, and tux before, although I usually included them whenever I did the packing. The moment, it seemed, had finally arrived. He held up his arms in a modeling pose.

"Well, what do you think? Does it still fit?"

"To perfection," I declared with a touch of envy. "If it were mine, I'd have gone through four sizes by now."

"Actually," Geoff picked up the thread of our conversation as he plucked lint from the jacket, "that fellow Skully might not even exist. Rodriguez could have represented non-existent Skully in the realtor's office. He could have represented himself as Skully's salesman in the store. The one thing he couldn't do was represent himself as Skully when applying for the pass into the book stacks since Skully isn't a Latin name. Men who scheme murder try to keep witnesses and accomplices to a minimum. I won't be at all surprised tomorrow if we find the realtor never actually saw Skully."

Weston began slowly pacing the length of the room, gradually accelerating his walk. "No, that won't surprise me. A matter more to the point is why Rodriguez took out a pass at all. The whole front of the library is occupied by galleries, offices and a reading room. The book stacks don't extend that far at all."

80

"Perhaps," I conjectured as I set aside the pass and stuck the neolite shavings under my lens, "the fellow opened one of the upper windows in the stacks and climbed to the roof from there."

Weston continued to wear a groove in the rug as he trekked across our combination living room-kitchen.

"No, John, that simply won't do. One of the guards told me those windows are nailed shut to protect the collections from rain and theft. A pried-open window would have been noticed. What's more, there are much easier ways to gain access to the roof, for whatever purpose. When it comes right down to it, since we don't know yet how the murder was committed, we can't even be sure the assassin needed to get onto the roof."

"Then perhaps," I theorized, "the murderer went into the stacks to steal something. Well, not actually steal . . . with all those seventy odd million volumes he could have intentionally misshelved certain kinds of books and they wouldn't have been found for years. He could have been hiding some crucial piece of information from Senators Strong and Kidd. They found out about it anyway, so he killed them."

"Not seventy million *books*," Geoff corrected. "You're counting all the collections and the microfilm. But you make a good point. Except . . . what's the date on that card?"

I applied some solution to the upper right hand corner and waited for the letters to develop.

"January fifteenth to February fifteenth seems to be the life of the pass."

"Then," Geoff snapped, "the murderer entered the stacks after he'd already sold Strong the shoes. If he already planned to kill him, why hide any books? Even if the killing itself was a contingency plan, one would expect the censorship to take place first."

"Unless," I noted, "the murder was planned from the beginning but for some reason had to be delayed. Perhaps some of their machinery malfunctioned. Burying books

81

might, therefore, be a contingency designed to sidetrack Strong until the murder became possible."

Geoff slowed momentarily. "Yes, that would explain a lot. I can't help feeling, though, that we don't quite have a handle yet on what happened."

"It is rather frustrating," I agreed. "We haven't faced a more baffling puzzle since Paloma's brother was kidnapped over the tele. And it took the NASA computer to help figure that one out."

My partner appeared suddenly quite preoccupied.

"Yes, of course. The tele case. Transmissions from across the street. Transmission . . . . Transmission towers . . . . Good grief! It's so simple. That's got to be what happened! I could kick myself for not seeing it sooner."

"For not seeing what?"

"How Strong was murdered."

"And how was that?"

Instead of answering, Weston hurried over to the telephone stand and thumbed frantically through the front of a directory.

"Yes, here it is. 555-7272." He spun the rotary dial with quick, jerky movements, pressed the receiver to his ear and listened. As he stood there, he began gradually to relax. Apparently satisfied at last, he slammed the receiver back into its cradle.

"Good," he declared, "we've got a little time."

"A little time for what?"

He resumed his pacing but at a decidedly more leisurely rate.

"To prevent the next murder, old bean."

"The *next* one!"

"But of course. There might be hundreds more planned. I should have realized that at least an hour ago. All the evidence was there. I suppose I was just too preoccupied with the need for self-defense. Now the problem is to formulate some way to prevent the slaughter. You finish

relaxed to the point of laying her purse and propaganda beside her. I noticed with considerable relief that, in spite of the apartment's warmth, she didn't unbutton her loose-fitting sweater. Perhaps the visit wouldn't last long.

"I'm afraid," Weston admitted as he eased into one of the arm chairs across from her, "we are rather new in the neighborhood. Now, you were saying about the world?"

Miss Vickers cleared her throat. "I was saying...." She cleared her throat again and coughed. "Do you mind if I get a drink of water before we start?"

By that time I was already descending into the other chair but caught myself by pushing down on its arms.

"Why of course not, madam. I'll get..."

She gestured for me to sit. "No, no. Don't bother. The dishrack's full of glasses. I'll get it myself."

I re-reversed directions and sank into the cushions. "As you wish."

She hurried over to the sink amidst a torrent of coughs while I stared a dagger or two in Geoff's direction. We simply hadn't the time to spare for this! My partner seemed totally at ease while we waited, but I felt somewhat uneasy. The woman was rather nondescript, neither plain nor pretty, though her round face did have a certain charm to it. She wasn't threatening in the least, but an indefinable something about her made the hairs on the back of my neck stand on end. After downing a full two glasses of water, she came back across the room and resumed her perch on the sofa.

"I'm sorry, gentlemen, for the interruption." She paused for one final cough. "Between the night air and all the talking, it's a wonder I have any voice left at all. I talk, of course, because I have such marvelous news. Did you know that the time is coming when the lion and the lamb will lie down together right here on earth! Swords will be beaten into plowshares and there won't be any more wars!"

"Why yes, of course," my partner agreed. "Just a little after that, as I recall, every knee shall bow and every tongue confess Jesus as Lord."

85

She ignored his reply and picked up one of her magazines as a prop.

"There are some articles in here," she informed us, "which show how today's events fit into the Old and New Testament prophecies. The wars, the rumors of wars, the . . . . "

"Nineteen fourteen was a good year for wars," Geoff quipped. "I seem to recall your leaders predicted Christ would return that year, then covered their blunder by semantic juggling. I'd much prefer you dismounted your hobbyhorse and stopped gushing the party line. Dare to think for yourself, and we might get somewhere."

Jane blinked, then took a deep breath. I half expected and hoped that she'd get right up and leave since it was obvious she'd make no converts here. Geoff's confrontation tactics, however, failed to completely dissolve her composure.

"If you attended any of our gatherings," she assured him with forced smoothness, "you'd realize we don't just passively accept kingdom teaching. Our group contains doctors, lawyers and others with inquiring minds, and I'll have you know we take a more active part in our meetings than the members of protestant churches do."

"Ah," Geoff responded, "but I *have* attended. You're right, of course, about the activity level, but what I saw was all carefully programmed to give the mere illusion of freedom. B.F. Skinner himself would be impressed by your techniques. He, you'll remember, is the psychologist who specialized in training rats."

Our visitor patted her frizzy hairdo without altering its configuration one millimeter.

"I'm well acquainted," she informed us archly, "with B.F. Skinner. I wish you were half as well informed about us. People are always spreading lies or jumping to unfounded conclusions. I'm afraid you've done exactly that by sitting in on something you didn't really understand."

Weston paused to pick a previously overlooked piece of lint from his jacket.

"When I attended," he commented matter-of-factly, "a

86

leader stood up front and asked questions from a book. The congregation then raced to see who could look up the answers first in their copies. The winner received the glorious privilege and social coup of reading the officially approved answer aloud. Then, there were easy chairs up front so that a woman, who wasn't permitted to teach men, could, in the best Pharisaical tradition teach *before* men while pretending to be sitting in an unbeliever's living room. Am I jumping at any unfounded conclusions? And, oh yes, there was also a designated time when anyone could stand up and say a few words. I don't know what happens after that because when I stood up to say that the word translated 'Lord' in the New Testament is the same word in the ancient Greek translation of the Old Testament translated Yaweh, your intellectually curious, open-minded friends bodily threw me out. They didn't seem particularly happy about translating Romans 10:9, 'that if you confess with your mouth Jesus as Jehovah and believe in your heart that God raised Him from the dead, you shall be saved.' "

Jane crossed her legs and managed an iron smile as she visualized the sight.

"You can't blame them for that, can you? Your translation has God raising God from the dead. There's only one God, not two. But let's not get into that subject. I'm the one visiting so I should be able to say what I've come for. You can talk to me all you want about other matters when you knock on my door."

"Which," Geoff completed, "you've learned from experience is unlikely since I'm not supplied with a quota of hours for house-to-house work nor am I paid a salary for it as some of your people are. In point of fact, madam, you have obligations as a guest in this house and one of them is to be flexible enough to lay aside the material you parrot and chat about whatever interests me. I'll do the same when I visit you since I consider it a matter of common courtesy. In the book of Job even Satan talked about what his host Jehovah wanted to discuss when he visited God in heaven. Take a lesson in courtesy from the devil."

I'd never seen a Jehovah's Witness become angry before. Generally they simply smiled and backed off. Jane's clenching and unclenching fists and her set jaw were evidence though that Geoff had finally pushed this lady over the edge.

"Mr. Weston," she exploded, "I think that's exactly what I am doing by listening to you. You've no right to compare my visit here with the devil visiting God. I'm no Satanic ally and you're certainly no god—except of the 'little tin' variety. You're the most uncouth, exasperating person I've ever met."

Geoff relaxed and grinned from ear to ear. "Now that," he observed approvingly, "is more like it. I prefer honest hostility to hypocritical sweetness any day, and it's certainly nice to see you abandon your script. I hate to talk with someone whose every answer has been publicly rehearsed.

"So I'm the devil, am I? Let's deal with that. It is you, of course, who drew the parallel between yourself and Satan. I merely suggested you emulate good manners. I can see, however, how you'd jump to the conclusion that I was calling you demonic because you've considered me that all along. A churchman—and an evangelical like myself—must be highly suspect. You've simply projected your own antagonistic feelings upon me."

Jane's hands were still clenched and turning white at the knuckles. I could almost see her counting under her breath while trying to regain control. Since Geoff approved of her anger, she seemed determined to stifle it, yet to be the more infuriated by his very approval.

"If," she declared with barely suppressed venom, "my friend Susan weren't sick tonight, you'd have a real debate on your hands. She's a better speaker than I am. I'll say this, though. To smile and agree occasionally with somebody isn't hypocrisy. It's the same good manners you *claim* to value. Isn't it your people who are so fond of saying 'hate the sin but love the sinner' and that 'unbelievers' are 'of their father the

88

devil'? I, too, can despise a system but love its victims. My methods aren't any different from yours."

"No different," Weston shot back, "except that I don't consider everyone outside my own church an 'unbeliever' as you do. And when I love someone, I show that love by telling him how he's been victimized rather than by insinuating myself into his good graces and gradually subverting his beliefs." A twinkle lurked in Geoff's eyes. "It's nice to know, though, that you love me."

Our visitor eyed Weston with two hundred proof distilled hatred.

"Perhaps," I interjected as referee, "if you two would concentrate less on personal attacks and more on doctrine we could...."

"An excellent idea," Weston interrupted. "After all, the woman has been avoiding the subject of Christ's deity."

"Avoiding!" Jane's voice cracked. "I've been too busy defending myself to even bring it up. But let's do just that. The whole idea of the trinity's so nonsensical that I don't see how any rational person could accept it. Three doesn't equal one. There can't be three infinite gods who are somehow united. God isn't some multi-headed monster, and he certainly can't be one yet more than one at the same time."

Weston pulled a bag of peanuts from his tuxedo jacket pocket.

"Your scientific reasoning is impeccable," he concluded, "provided one rejects Newton's invention of calculus in the seventeenth century and almost every mathematical advance since then. Madam, there can be an infinity of infinities. That is a mathematical fact. And even Newton's idea of tiny particles which simultaneously do and don't exist has recently been resurrected. Science itself becomes a study of paradox at the subatomic level. So why can't the *inventor* of the subatomic display that same freedom from your puny logic? If matter can be zero and more than zero at the same time, surely God can be one and three. Your problem is that you have the same simplistic view of the world Albert

Einstein had. You refuse to accept mystery."

"I would say," Jane rebutted scornfully, "that I'm in pretty good company if Einstein agrees with me. No matter what you say, more than one isn't one! That's a logical absurdity!"

Weston tore the cellophane wrapper and popped some peanuts into his mouth.

"By *our* limited logic I suppose it is. But then, our logic is bound by four dimensions while Newton's tiny specks evidently shade into higher realms we can't comprehend. So do the light particle bundles Einstein envisioned while trying to explain why light acts as both a wave and a particle. Did you know, madam, that if you measure a light wave bending around a star, the light bends around both sides? But if you measure the same light as a particle, it comes around only one side? It's in either two places at the same time or in one of them without being there! Did you know that after Einstein's death someone experimented with his theories and found that contrary to Einstein's predictions, when part of a split particle of light passed through a polarizing filter, its other half automatically polarized as well. The two separate, distinct particles moving in opposite directions at tremendous speed *were actually one!*

"Now, if a light particle can be two when measured as a wave but one as a particle, and may be split into two but still act as one and remain one, then I personally have no problem with the trinity! Christ is one with the Father but a distinct person acting together with Him. The Holy Spirit enjoys the same relationship with the Father and the Son."

Jane stared holes through Weston. "I don't," she declared, "believe a word you've said."

"That," Weston assured her, "is entirely your prerogative. But if you face reality as reality, you've got to reconsider your logic. The passages in Hebrews 5 and the second Psalm, for example . . ."

"Excuse me," Jane interrupted, "could you tell me where the bathroom is. I shouldn't have drunk all that water."

"Why, yes," I responded helpfully, "it's down the hallway, first door to the left."

"Thank you."

She abandoned her purse and stack of magazines on the sofa and beat a hasty retreat from the scene of battle.

I glanced reproachfully at Geoff. "Old bean," I scolded, "you are being a might hard on the lady. I don't condone her teaching either, but..."

My voice trailed off. I couldn't believe my eyes. No sooner had the bathroom door closed when Weston stepped quickly over to the sofa and began going through our visitor's purse. As he leafed through her wallet, he gestured in circles for me to keep talking.

"...I mean..." I contorted my face into a silent appeal for an explanation, "you're not... debating fairly. First you attack her organization, then you argue doctrine on so high a level that the poor thing doesn't even understand you."

Geoff found her driver's license, removed it and stuffed it in his pocket. As we heard the toilet flush, he put the wallet back in her purse and quickly returned to his seat. Not over a second later the bathroom door opened and our 'guest' stalked out swishing her floor-length dress.

"As you've said yourself," she remarked with chilly self-control, "we have a different set of presuppositions, so there's no point in our talking further. Besides, it's getting late and I have to be going." She paused to retrieve her bundle of magazines and marched to the door. Before Geoff could even reach out for the knob, she jerked the door open and slammed it closed behind her. I could just make out the sound of footsteps clacking not very daintily down the corridor.

"My word," I breathed, "what's going on here, anyway? Why all the intimidation? Why did you steal her license?"

"Steal," Geoff repeated soberly, "now that's an ugly word. I just rescued Amy Sheldon's permit from our self-proclaimed Jane Vickers. The woman's an imposter. As soon as she steps outside the main entrance we're going places. I

91

only hope she's rattled enough that she doesn't notice she's got a tail."

When the clacking stopped, we eased out into the hallway and hurried to the street. Our Cadillac was located almost directly in front of the apartment house, so we trotted across the sidewalk while keeping an eye on the woman's departing figure. We needn't have worried. By this time she was halfway down the block and, if anything, accelerating her pace. She never thought to look back. Geoff had most definitely lit a fire under her. I only hoped her motorcar wasn't parked too far away. We'd be a might suspicious following a pedestrian while driving six miles per hour, and if we followed on foot, she'd be sure to find transportation and give us the slip. I kept an eye on her while Weston hurried to the driver's side and switched off the fender burglar alarm. I noted impatiently that the woman had stopped by a car and was fumbling for her keys.

"Hurry up, old chap," I conveyed agitatedly. "She's about to get away. She's..."

I saw Geoff's pocket torch flash on, then quickly off again. After that, instead of unlocking the motorcar, he walked slowly back around to my side. I didn't have to ask what the matter was. The street lamp threw just enough light our way so I could make out the consternation on his face.

"The toothpick," he commented without inflection, "has been dislodged from the door." He paused. "In the heat of the chase I almost didn't stop to check. The murderer almost succeeded. Let's go back inside and find out what goodies Miss Sheldon-Vickers has planted in our quarters."

Just then the sound of squealing tires heralded our guest's departure. Her sports coupe roared through first and second gears and was still picking up speed as it ran through the yellow light on the next corner.

Our apartment seemed very peaceful now that the sounds of verbal combat had faded. Yet both Weston and I remained apprehensive. We felt rather like we were tiptoeing through a minefield.

"Well," I commented as I paced the living room with my bug detector, "at least we know she didn't put blowfish poison on the doorknobs."

Weston was scrutinizing the fabric of each sofa cushion inch by inch under his magnifying lens.

"We do, indeed," he noted with abstract detachment. "If she had, we'd be a couple of zombies by now. It's a good thing our murderer isn't a Haitian witch doctor."

"Yes," I agreed, "I guess it is. But what I don't understand is how you knew Miss Vickers was a fraud. What did she do to make you catch on?"

Geoff pulled the cushion off and held his torch so he could examine the recess behind it.

"I suppose," he observed, "her first mistake was to knock on the door across the hall. No one's living there, so she came directly over here. That seemed highly suspicious to me since there are four other apartments on this floor. Why didn't she take each in turn? Then I remembered that only two of the six lacked a name on their vestibule mailbox—ours and the flat across the way. Either the woman made a hobby of visiting vacant lodgings or she was looking for new tenants. Now, if I knew two foreigners had left the Library of Congress carrying luggage but showed up later on Capitol Hill with narry a suitcase, I'd probably start canvassing the immediate neighborhood looking for new renters. Suppose I'd done my homework and knew that that chap Weston had a reputation for enjoying religious arguments. What better disguise could I choose for my operative than that of a Jehovah's Witness? The woman wouldn't arouse suspicion going door to door and would stand a good chance of getting in once she found us."

I upended the coffee table to check underneath. All I found for my trouble was cheap pressboard. Neither bomb nor bug was glued anywhere.

"Then why," I wondered aloud, "did she show up so late on

our doorstep? We're only a couple of blocks from the library. Surely it wouldn't take that long to locate us."

"Ah, but the murderer had a lot to occupy him. He either had to give someone a crash course in kingdom theology so she could play the part or, more probably, find a past or present Jehovah's Witness who was willing to cooperate. Then there was the matter of coming at an hour when tenants were likely to be home. Every apartment door that didn't open had to be revisited periodically. I'm not surprised it took a little while. What did surprise me, though, was the clumsiness of the effort."

Geoff finished scanning the sofa arm for poisoned needles and such. He bent low to check underneath where "Jane" could have kicked any object hidden under her skirt. Then, apparently satisfied, he retraced the steps our visitor had taken to the sink.

"I wasn't aware," I admitted, "that the act was all that bungling. I didn't see . . . "

"Precisely," Weston cut me off. "You didn't listen either." He stuck his head into the sink cabinet but continued speaking amidst somewhat cave-like harmonics. "When the woman started speaking in the hall she was entirely too eager to gain entrance to our quarters. Witnesses don't press for that. And unaccompanied women are not particularly eager to step behind closed doors with strange men. The very fact that she was unaccompanied was a dead giveaway. J.W.'s travel in pairs."

"But," I pointed out, "she explained that her partner was ill."

The sound of banging pots emanated from under the sink.

"She said it," Geoff confirmed. "She had to say something. Her very attempt at explaining, however, put her in a worse light. J.W.'s use an apprentice system, teaming seasoned veterans with neophytes. I know that because I always identify the neophyte and aim the hardest questions his way to shake things up a might. Now who was the neophyte in Jane's team? If *she* were, she'd hardly go out alone even in an emergency. Yet she claimed—to cover any shortcomings on her part—that her partner was the superior debater. No, old chap, her motive for coming alone was so that there'd be one less witness to her crime."

I groaned inwardly at the pun.

"Which crime," I observed, "doesn't seem to include bugging." I stepped over to the kitchen and quickly scanned the area with my radio wave detector. The results were negative. "I'll have a go at the hall and bathroom on the off chance. Be back in a moment."

"Be careful for booby traps," the voice in the cabinet warned. "That woman could have retreated from the conversation anytime she wanted. She was totally out of character in staying as long as she did. I think she hung around so she could claim those drinks had taken effect and go plant something in the bathroom. Notice how quickly she wanted to leave after that little visit."

"It all sounds plausible," I admitted, "but I think you may have read in sinister intent when there was none. The woman could have been an unusually advanced neophyte who used a phony name to prevent telephone harassment by anyone she visited. She . . . "

" . . . was an assassin," Geoff finished with finality. "Her last and biggest blunder was to call me by name in the heat of argument. How did she know it? It wasn't on the mailbox. We didn't tell her. Our faces don't exactly have celebrity status in this country. Explain that away."

I couldn't, of course, so I remained silent and went about my work. No one's ever approached a bathroom more gingerly than I. Fortunately, Amy Sheldon, alias Jane Vickers, hadn't closed that door when she left. If she had, I doubt I'd have entered for fear of a jamb-activated bomb. Since it was open, however, I fairly tiptoed in and took a quick check for bugs. Nothing. The murderer wasn't concerned with knowing our plans. That could only mean he didn't think we'd live long enough to carry them out and didn't want telltale bugs lying around the murder scene.

I pocketed my snooper and set about giving the place a once over. The commode was, of course, the logical place to start. Explosives in the tank could be activated by pushing the flush handle or—I swallowed hard—by lifting the tank lid. Since I didn't have a ceramic drill handy, however, there didn't seem to be much choice. I tore a sheet from my note pad, raised the lid ever so slightly and slid the paper halfway into the crack. I then carefully worked the sheet around the entire perimeter searching for obstructions. So far as I could determine there were none. I lifted the lid ever so gently from its retaining notch and slid it forward until . . . the enclosure was empty. Now where else could something be secreted? There was no vanity cabinet, only a sink clinging to the wall. Perhaps underneath its rim? I knelt down and twisted into a pretzel to have a look upward. Nothing. There wasn't any toothpaste, so a poisoned tube such as we'd encountered in the Maltese treasure case was out. Could there be contact poison on the soap or a snake in the medicine cabinet? I reached out tentatively toward the mirrored chest.

"John!" Weston's voice boomed from the other room. "Come have a look at this. You may find it helpful."

With a touch of relief I left the door unopened and hurried back out to the kitchen nook. Geoff, I discovered, was involved with a mirror of his own, a hand-held one which he had positioned under the sink faucet.

"I've unscrewed the rust screen from the spigot," he informed me without looking up. "I'm not the first to have done so, either. Notice what's been shoved up in there."

He gave me charge of the reflector and I slanted it to accommodate my angle.

"Oh ho!" I breathed, "it looks like a white Life Saver confection with hooks protruding outward from the rim to snag the pipe."

"A life saver in appearance," Weston concurred, "but certainly not in effect. It's got to be some kind of poison in a waxy base, some extremely potent chemical that would prove effective in even minute, time-released doses. Care to make any guesses?"

"Well," I mused, "there was a substance developed during World War II so powerful that a single ounce could kill America's total population. Our murderer's organization might hesitate to handle something that deadly, though. Lead compounds might drive us as mad as they did Nero, but I doubt they'd be potent or fast enough. There's always arsenic trioxide. It's the same white color and totally tasteless." I put my nose to the faucet and sniffed. "One thing's certain. It's not cyanide."

"No," Geoff agreed, "it's not. I'm inclined to doubt *any* of the more traditional poisons, though, on general principles. Our murderer appears rather inventive as well as bent on making our deaths seem accidental."

"Up to the point," I corrected him, "where he had a bomb planted in our motorcar."

"If," Geoff reflected, "it was a traditional bomb. That, of course, was my first reaction but now I wonder. You know, the amazing thing about this case is that we've started with an almost total absence of clues and without the slightest official cooperation. The murderer must be either immensely vulnerable or vastly overconfident because he's supplied us with enough evidence, through trying to kill us, to involve the FBI, Secret Service, city police, county police, and even Metropol."

He savored the thought then scowled. "You check the bathroom water, then finish your search so we won't have any other deadly surprises. Our phone's probably tapped by now. I'll trot on down to the corner grocery to call homicide and update Washington's equivalent to Fleet Street. Within the hour, this place should be swarming with police and reporters. The lid will be off and our assassin should have less reason to silence us."

"You'd better call Paloma, too," I advised, "and cancel your date."

"Not on your life," Weston shot back. "We'll simply reschedule for midnight and ask her to supply the motorcar."

"If she agrees to *that*," I remarked, "I'll pick up the check—that is if we can find a restaurant still open. Your lack of timing or buckling of swash amazes me."

Geoff patted my shoulder as though I'd done something generous. "Thanks, old bean. The meal after that will be on me." He turned and quite literally trotted out the door. I combined a heavenward glance with a resigned sigh and then got back to work.

The newspaper reporters turned out to be just as brash and dogged as in London, if fewer in number. Their ranks were swelled, however, by an army of television journalists and cameramen. We were, it seemed, the rarest of all jewels, a fast-breaking news story just before airtime.

When I finished my chores and responded to the flashing lights and general pandemonium outside by following my nose to the front of the building, I was met with a battery of flashbulbs and a barrage of questions as a dozen otherwise rational people tried to poke a like number of microphones down my throat. Geoff was standing by one of the police cars, bathed in alternating blue and red beams and waxing eloquent in front of hungry interviewers while a uniformed and thoroughly disgruntled police lieutenant tried to get a word in edgewise.

Other officers were making a valiant effort to cordon off the area around our Cadillac while flak jacketed gentlemen, wearing what looked like steel welders' masks, searched under the bonnet and dash, ripped out the rear seat and invaded the trunk. As a crowd of curious neighbors pressed forward, cameramen now and again broke through the lines and blinded the workers with quartz light bars and popping strobe flashes. Meanwhile, every thirty seconds or so, another police cruiser braked to a halt amid the warble of siren and the angry honks of motorists trying to squeeze by a traffic jam which now included remote television broadcast vans from several commercial stations.

As I attempted to jostle my way toward the policeman in charge, a mike hit me in the front teeth and a cacophony of questions continued to assault me.

"Sir, are you Mr. Weston's assistant?"

I looked about for the questioner in the crowd but couldn't see her. "Yes, yes I am."

Another invisible questioner behind me pounced verbally. "How close did you come to boarding the ill-fated Concorde?"

I hadn't time to answer before others joined in.

"Could you tell our listeners how it felt to . . . "

"What kind of poison was planted in your . . . "

"Why do you think Senator Strong's death wasn't . . . "

"Has Middle East terrorism finally reached Washington?"

"How should I know?" I barked in answer to that one. "We haven't found the murderer yet, and anybody could have claimed . . . "

"You're rumored to be insolvent. Have you staged all this to earn a fee?"

I searched for a face to match the voice. "Who said that?"

"I did." The fellow had an unruly shock of red hair and camera-pleasing features. "It's rumored your bank account's overdrawn. What do you say to the charge you've fabricated evidence to . . . "

"I'd say," I shot back, "that you'd better do your homework. We have a savings account without cheque writing privileges. How does one overdraw that kind of account? Who are you, and when did you get the anonymous phone call?"

The reporter actually reddened. "Then you didn't . . . "

"Who are you, and when did you get the call?"

"Randall Shane from Eyewitness News. This afternoon."

"When," I pointed out, "the only people who knew we were in town were our client, a librarian, a couple of Senate employees, and the murderer. For your information, we have a substantial balance in our account. If we don't, then you'd better check for computer fraud because I keep duplicate written records which will back me up. Excuse me, gentlemen, I find there's a matter that needs my immediate attention."

I turned on my heels, shoved my way back to the building entrance, and hurried down the hall with the whole herd pressing behind as though I were lead buffalo in a stampede. With some difficulty, I finally managed to gain entrance to our flat and force the door closed behind me. There wasn't time to relax and enjoy the solitude, though. I stepped over to the phone and direct dialed a seemingly endless string of numbers. A series of beeps was followed by ringing on the other end.

"Scotland Yard."

"I'd like to speak with Inspector Twigg, please."

"Just a moment. Hold the line."

"Gladly."

After an interminable pause, there was a click followed by a gruff voice I'd have recognized anywhere.

"Twigg here. May I help you?"

"You certainly may," I responded. "This is John Taylor. Look, old friend, we're in a bit of a tight spot, and I need you to go out on a limb for us."

"With a name like Twigg," he chuckled, "how could I refuse. Seriously, though, I owe you lads a couple. If there's anything I can do . . . ."

"We're in Washington," I informed him, "and the assassin we're after may be trying to sabotage the investigation by tampering with our bank account. I've just mentioned publicly that I possess written records to discredit any computer tampering. Someone's going to want those records and they'll probably conclude they're in our quarters. Now don't say anything. This line may be tapped. You know where the records are. Put stakeouts at every location the murderer might suspect and guard those papers with your life."

"A bit of a stiff order that," he conceded, "but I think I can come up with the men."

"If you catch anybody," I warned him, "charge him with murder and try to prevent bond. You may have the chap who

100

bombed that Concorde. If not, the fellow knows him. And any robbery there is accessory-after-the-fact, murder one here. We have two dead Senators on our hands and if you let the blighter out of custody, it'll cause a bigger scandal than when those Italian blokes let the fellow loose after that ship hijacking."

"Understood." Twigg's manner was clipped. "If the Concorde's involved, we'll have half the force working this end."

"It's involved," I assured him. "We were supposed to be on that plane. You'd better move fast and radio teams into place. The organization we're up against has a super communication network. You've got to beat them to the punch."

"Then stop bending my ear," the inspector growled. He broke the connection, probably by slamming the receiver down on the hook.

The click on my end almost coincided with the turning of a key in the lock. Three patrolmen came tramping in followed by the lieutenant and my partner.

"The poison's in the kitchen spigot," Weston informed the work crew. "John can tell you where else."

"It's in every faucet as well as the shower head," I said. "There don't, however, seem to be any other nasty surprises. You're free to double check, of course."

The lieutenant was a giant of a man, fully six feet six, and must have weighed twenty stone. Except for his cleanshaven jaw and crew cut, he exactly fit my impression of a Viking warrior which I'm sure would have been high compliment to the Viking. I was more interested in the bagged wire tap transmitter he held, however, than in his stature. His men had been busy and their discovery meant my call had evidently escaped detection by our enemy.

Weston handed the lieutenant Amy Sheldon's laminated license.

"The woman," he commented dryly, "seemed a bit upset at my debate tactics. Put the lady under surveillance and you just might find her circle of acquaintances rather interesting."

"I'll get on it right away." His voice was deep and boomed with self-confident authority. "You are not, however, heading up this investigation. I disapprove of the circus antics I've seen here tonight. The department disapproves. And the department will remain in charge from now on!"

Weston smiled mischievously. "If you want to be in charge of circus antics," he deliberately misinterpreted, "then be my guest. You'll admit, though, it shows rather bad taste in such a serious case. I'll demonstrate for you tomorrow how Senator Strong was assassinated. Or should I do that for the FBI? No matter. John and I have to hurry off now for a most urgent conference. Our motorcar will, of course, be impounded as evidence. Let us know when it's released. The door bolt's spring loaded. Don't forget to lock up when you leave."

"You are not going anywhere," the lieutenant declared with conviction, "until I finish the questioning."

"Oh yes we are," Geoff shot back, "unless you arrest us. You are the public servant. We are the public. We'll gladly cooperate with you if you do so with us, but we won't waste time being ordered around needlessly. You have all the information you need. You have all the evidence we have. Use it. For me to say more would be to rake over old ground. Good day, sir. We really have to toddle along."

We left the lieutenant tongue-tied and stewing in his own juice as we walked briskly from the apartment on the way to our midnight rendezvous. Out front we passed a wrecker lorry lifting the Cadillac's rear end in preparation for a drive to the impound yard. As we left the reporters and the clamor behind, I noticed that the stars were shining brightly overhead. Two blocks further along a limosine awaited us in the spot that Geoff had designated when he called Blair House. The dinner was to be my treat.

8
GOOD NIGHT, IRENE

Geoff, the President's daughter, and I had last dined together atop the Latin American Tower with Mexico City's nighttime panorama glittering far below us. Now we were seated in a less elegant ship-shaped seafood restaurant by the Potomac. As I looked across the table at Paloma, however, I experienced a sense of *deja vu*, as though we were reliving the past. She hadn't changed at all. She had the same liquid brown eyes that so readily saw the good in people. Her fine features, sharp Castillian chin, and fair complexion were just as before. She'd trimmed her hair, but raven cascades still reached nearly to her waist. A diamond choker now graced her neck and sparkled all the lovelier before the backdrop of dark tresses. I remembered her as a simple dresser, favoring slacks and print blouses. Now she was wearing a lacy evening gown more suitable for walking the aisle as a bridesmaid than sitting in a booth with clam shells and a fish net pasted to the wall behind her. No, nothing had really changed. I could see why my partner was attracted to her.

"*Ay que, Geoff!*" Her voice was deep and lilting as she toasted him with her water glass. "May it not be another eternity before we meet again. I'm learning English to be able to use some in my letters, but I'd rather practice by speaking. You look very handsome in your suit. I've never seen you that way before."

"Neither," I intercepted the compliment, "has anybody else. Thank you for the miracle. You've brought the troglodyte out of the cave and suited him for society."

"Surely not I." She blushed sweetly. "After all, he's a world traveler."

"Gathering 'cluebuds' while he may," Weston alluded to Herrick's poem. "No, I'm afraid John's quite right. I'm far too preoccupied with work and tend to neglect the social amenities. It's nice to be out with you tonight. I've looked forward to it."

"So have I," she admitted.

The waitress, who had already taken our orders, glided our way with a tray full of cups and began dispensing coffee from a carafe. I took mine with cream. Geoff opted for black, and Paloma added creamed coffee to her sugar.

"You might also," I addressed the attendant, "take some coffee over to those two gentlemen in the corner and put it on our bill." I pointed unobtrusively toward the Secret Service agents at another table.

"Yes, sir." She started to leave, then turned back uncertainly. "Shall I tell them you all are buying?"

"They'll know," Weston interceded.

"But don't be obvious about it," I added. "They'd rather not be identified as members of our party."

"Of course." The woman seemed puzzled and quite curious, but she hurried to comply.

Geoff buttered a roll from the courtesy basket and perched it on his saucer rim. We'd already said grace.

"Now," he prompted Paloma, "tell us about that attempt on your life."

"There isn't much to tell." She stirred the coffee and tried a spoonful of the steamy brew. "A friend and I were on our way to Bellas Artes for a concert when a car pulled up beside us at a stoplight. We have bulletproof glass in the limosine, but the air conditioner wasn't working. The windows were partway down. The driver was hit before we could close up. But he's had anti-terrorist training and managed to get us away to safety before he collapsed."

"Where," Geoff prompted, "were the bullet holes?"

"On the rear door and window and inside the rear compartment. I think that's why Jose survived. They were shooting at me."

104

"Or," I corrected, "at your companion."

"I can't believe that." She blew on her spoon before trying another sip. "Gabriel is a graduate student at the university. He's not interested in politics at all, *ni un poquito*. When he graduates he's going to manage his father's shoe factory."

Weston's eyebrows raised almost imperceptively. "That would be Gabriel...?"

"Delgado Soto."

"And his father is..."

"Ricardo. He's president of Comodo Shoes."

"And the papa has no political ties either?"

"Not that I know of. Of course he's a supporter of PRI, the Revolutionary Independent Party, as most businessmen are, but he's never run for office that I can remember."

"If," I interjected, "you were the intended victim, give us your best guess as to motive. Obviously the usual kidnapping for ransom is out unless your assailants were incredibly bad shots."

She considered as she spread her napkin on her lap.

"Of course I've been thinking about that, but I can't answer with certainty. It could be communist terrorism. As you may or may not know, the rebels from Central America have been crossing over into southern Mexico. At first we pretended they weren't there because we didn't want to admit we couldn't defend our own frontier. It's a very wild area, and we've never even controlled banditry there. Now the rebels have set up permanent bases and are pushing north. First they side with Catholic extremists against the protestants. When the evangelicals are killed, then they terrorize the *alcaldes*, our mayors, and the extremists. My father's been moving troops south in hopes of crushing the rebels. He's also been getting threats from both the guerillas and members of the local communist party. If those were the only death notes he got, the solution would be simple, wouldn't it?"

I nodded but said nothing.

"However, there have also," she continued, "been

warnings from other sources and we're not quite sure from whom. It could be almost any group. You know that for years our economy has been struggling. It is, of course, common knowledge. We borrowed heavily with petroleum reserves as collateral and then oil prices plummeted. Graft kept the borrowed money from being used effectively and interest began systematically draining our country's vitality. That earthquake a few years back didn't help either. Even after all this time, we're still paying mostly interest, and angry voices are demanding we renounce our debts."

"But that," Weston pointed out, "would most certainly be followed by other renunciations and the biggest banking collapse in history."

She lowered her dark eyelashes for just a second.

"I know. Why do you think my father resists the idea? Nearly all the big U.S. banks would fold and so would quite a few European institutions. That would mean depression throughout the West, and Mexico certainly wouldn't be exempt. Our commerce would be strangled for lack of credit. Remaining banks would refuse our accounts. The peso would devalue to nothing. Every affected country would slap trade embargoes on us. Whether we like it or not, our economy is tied to that of the United States; and if the U.S. reels, we die of convulsions."

"Then," I observed reasonably, "why the outcry to renounce?"

"Because people are frustrated and aren't thinking clearly. It's easy to see the lenders as villains since they nearly thrust the money into our hot little hands. Then, too, there are those who listen to the Cubanos and would gladly pull down the walls on the Americans even if we, like Samson, died in the wreckage. My father has been quietly negotiating with the banks to forgive future interest so that we can finally repay the principle. Because of that, some of our people call him a traitor. What makes matters worse is that the banks won't listen and have played right into the propagandists' hands. The institutions think daddy is fabricating the renunciation movement as a pressure tactic against them and don't realize he's fighting for their very existence."

"So," Geoff concluded, "we're left with you being shot at by communists, nationalists, bankers, anti-Americans, anti-protestants of whatever stripe, or someone with a grudge against a shoe company. How eclectic an array of suspects! You know, ever since I've known you, your family has had an amazing ability to attract thugs and assassins. During our first case together your brother's bodyguard was kidnapped and murdered. Then your brother was spirited out of the palace to nearly be killed, and your father was shaken down for a fortune. Now your chauffeur's been wounded, your father threatened and a shot or two directed your way." My partner smiled. "Do you think it's safe for me to associate with you?"

There was a pixie glint in Paloma's eyes. "Probably not," she bantered, "but I have the country's finest bodyguards. I'll ask them to defend you, too. We can also pray for each other. If God wants us together, He can protect us. But you sounded so heroic in your letters. I thought you would fight your way through a jungle just to pluck an orchid for my hair."

"Literary heroes," I said jovially, "are a might like actors on a cinemascope screen. I'm afraid they shrink when seen in person. In this case, though, I believe Geoff's real concern is your own safety, though he's kicking me under the table for saying so. You realize that detectives aren't exactly a cloistered lot and we make enemies."

The girl contemplated Geoff in all seriousness. "I am not afraid. Even if I were, I could never avoid you, for that would be to die in little pieces at the hands of an assassin's threats. Danger is a part of life, and I don't wish to run from it. What's more, I'm in danger anyway. Perhaps you will save my life."

Weston nodded thoughtfully. "Perhaps. By the way," he changed the subject, "how would your country be affected if everyone currently on U.S. welfare received $50,000 as investment capital?"

We were interrupted by the waitress who deftly balanced her tray while she set steamy platters of food before us.

Paloma skewered a crab ball while she considered Geoff's question.

"I think," she concluded, "such a handout would be something positive for us. Some of our people are here on forged papers and a percentage undoubtedly receive welfare. They'd probably bring the money back to Mexico to start a business. Naturalized citizens might send some, too, to relatives. And if the measure created more U.S. jobs, we'd get our share. Even a holographic national identity card hasn't completely stopped illegal entry, you know, just slowed it. As long as our unemployment is up, we welcome an escape valve—unofficially, of course."

"What," I interposed, "would be your response to the senators who oppose giving Mexico that military aid package?"

She paused before replying. "It would be to point out their nearsightedness. How could we afford to buy the arms when we're being sucked dry paying interest to American banks? How can we defend the country without weapons when the rebels are generously supplied through Nicaragua and Cuba? It's only a thousand kilometers from Oaxaca to Brownsville, Texas. If they don't help us defend Oaxaca today, they'll be defending Brownsville, McAllen and Laredo alone tomorrow."

I sampled a slice of flounder dipped in tartar sauce.

"If," I managed between bites, "the threat is really serious. I can see some wags claiming you've concocted the war to get supplies for your army so you can defend your northern borders after renouncing your debts."

Anger flashed momentarily in Paloma's eyes. "That vile rumor first appeared in *Pravda*. Consider the source! The International Red Cross works with our Cruz Roja. All anyone has to do is ask them for casualty statistics and he'll see how real the war is."

She softened a bit. "Besides, an invasion by the U.S. is probably the best thing that could happen to us. If they invaded, we'd get foreign aid. If they annexed us outright and created several new states, half our country would go on welfare and our PRI party would control the balance of power between Republicans and Democrats. Only our pride would be hurt, and we'd recover from that. What's more, the only way the Americans could collect their money would be to grant us an interest-free loan to pay off the banks and then build us up to help pay themselves back. They'd end up doing for us what daddy's trying to get the banks to do right now!"

"You sound," Weston noted admiringly, "more like an economist than a fine arts graduate."

"I sit at dinner with my father and his visitors," she stated simply. "In our family that's quite an honor. Daughters usually eat in the kitchen."

"And an honor well deserved," I commented. "Your observations have been most interesting. Have you, perhaps, talked along similar lines with Gabriel?"

"No." She stirred her coffee a few unnecessary times. "The man has a comic book/disco mentality. Every now and then I let him take me to hear the National Symphony and I relieve his boredom by telling him about Christ. We get into an argument, and I don't see him again for a couple of months. I think his father expects us to go together, so he keeps coming back for more.

"Let's not talk about me anymore, though. My life isn't all that interesting. I study. I design costumes for the Ballet Folklorico. You two are the ones who do the work that really matters. I've been brimming over with curiosity ever since you called. What new crimes are you solving? Are you in danger? Is that why there's been so much talk of assassins?" She continued in the plural but directed her attention to Geoff.

"I realize that all of life involves trusting God and taking risks, but sometimes I worry about you anyway because I know that, unlike me, you do not have a bodyguard."

"Your concern," Geoff noted sincerely, "is very precious to us. I wish we could set your mind at ease by telling you of all the precautions we're taking. Most of what we're doing is, of course, confidential. We simply can't discuss it." He sliced off a piece of crab cake while considering his next words. "I can say, though, that there could be a connection between a couple of murders we're looking into here and the attempt on your life. Don't think for a moment that you're out of danger just because you've put a few miles between yourself and Mexico City. Be extra careful."

She pushed an errant lock of hair back over her shoulder and contemplated him soberly.

"I will," she promised. "It's nice to know you're as concerned about me as I am about you. I have been praying for you."

I stabbed a shrimp and dunked it in sauce as the two studied each other in eloquent silence. Finally I resolved to break the mood.

"For that matter," I interjected, "I'm concerned for both of you. Eat up while your meal's still warm. You've plenty of time to become reacquainted later."

"Yes, quite!" Weston seized the opportunity. "Paloma, would you care to accompany me to a play or concert tomorrow night?"

She dazzled him with a smile. "A play sounds delightful. You can translate for me when the dialogue moves too fast for my English."

At that moment I could have kicked myself for being a royal fool. Here we were in the middle of a case and I'd just virtually arranged a date between Geoff and one of the suspects! Oh, she seemed all right. They'd been corresponding regularly for months. She was an intelligent, artistic, kind-hearted person. I liked her. But what Geoff was doing was just plain bad policy. He hadn't been aggressive in interrogating her a few moments ago. I'd asked the really tough questions. Now he was going to take her out for an evening's entertainment while a methodical killer stalked us both. I shuddered inwardly and set to devouring the food before me with a vengeance.

The rest of the meal was spent in small talk about Paloma's brother, my fiancee, June Albey, rugby, football, and the history of music from the elegance of Hayden, Beethoven and Tchaikovsky to the arid dissonance of Schonberg. Paloma held up her end of the conversation well and actually persuaded my partner to amend a couple of his opinions. Now that was a sight to see! I began to wonder if this *was* Weston's Irene Adler. She certainly had her wits about her. I also remembered how Irene had treated Holmes and it bothered me. We didn't head for home until nearly three a.m.

9
RECREATING A MURDER

I was at the bottom of a warm, peaceful pond floating weightlessly in dark oblivion. The quiet was so thick it produced a gentle ringing in my ears. Then the ringing reshaped into muffled, metallic sounds, and I began to rise. Slowly at first, then the lift increased until I was speeding to the surface like some giant cork unleashed from the depths. I broke through the surface, struggling to stay afloat. I found myself lying on a bed entangled in two layers of blankets and kicking for dear life. Geoff's voice carried clearly from the living room.

"Yes, Senator Grimes, I'd be happy to take custody of your shoes. Send a messenger right over, and make sure he's carrying identification. There are about ten policemen outside, and he'll have to run the gauntlet. Come by yourself in two hours, and I'll demonstrate just how close you came to being killed. Thank you for calling. Toodaloo."

As I stifled a yawn and struggled to a sitting position on the edge of the bed, the telephone jangled again.

"Hallo. Representative Davis' office? You do? When did you buy . . . I see. Well, send them over. No, I'm not afraid our apartment will be struck. Glad to be rid of them, are you? That's quite understandable. Come by at noon and we'll explain the mystery. Yes. Good day."

The clank of the phone hitting its cradle was followed immediately by an officious knock on the door. With considerable haste I gathered my clothes together and trotted for the bathroom feeling rather like a fireman late for a call. I hurried through a steamy shower, half dried myself, and fairly jumped into my suit. On entering the living area,

112

however, I found Geoff quite alone by the sink, peeling shoes with a carpet knife. Indeed, there was a sizable pile of footwear by the entrance, all neatly tagged. A wooden rectangular crate threatened to crush the coffee table. My partner had evidently been busy while I slept! I noticed a stack of newspapers on the kitchen table and headed over for a look.

"There's tea brewing on the stove," Geoff volunteered. "I couldn't get a decent blend of loose, but the bags aren't bad."

"In due time." I glanced down at the *Post* headline and article headings.

CONGRESS UNDER ATTACK!
"Poison Suspect Dies Under Questioning"
"Concorde Bombing Linked to Senate Assassinations"
"Alleged Bombers Killed in Shootout"

Accounts of our investigation covered virtually the entire first page. I peeled the *Post* off the stack and found much the same in the *Baltimore Sun*. We had apparently made quite a splash. I flipped back to the *Post* to study those articles which promised new information.

"Alleged Bombers Killed in Shootout"
Three suspected terrorists were killed last night in London and a fourth injured when they were surprised by police while burglarizing the offices of Sleuths Ltd., private investigators. According to informed sources, the quartet has been linked with the recent Concorde bombing which claimed the lives of 116 people. Efrain Guerra, the surviving gunman, has reportedly signed a statement and is speaking freely with police. Scotland Yard, however, isn't releasing any details pending further arrests.

A spokesman for Sleuths Ltd. theorizes that the four broke into the headquarters in an attempt to bankrupt the firm and impede its investigation of Senator Strong's and Senator Kidd's recent deaths. District of Columbia police had considered those fatalities the result of accidental lightning strikes until only yesterday. Now, however, both they and the FBI have shown renewed interest in the cases.

Meanwhile, Chief Clifford of the Montgomery County Police Department has announced formation of a special task force to investigate a hit-and-run attempt on the life of Geoffrey Weston and John Taylor, Sleuths Ltd. detectives. He hints that several related crimes in his jurisdiction tie the hit-and-run in with both senators' deaths. He stopped short, however, of referring to the lightning strikes as homicides.

Poison Suspect Dies Under Questioning

Congressional aide, Amy Sheldon, died this morning of a heart attack while being interrogated by District homicide squad detectives. She had just been formally charged with attempted murder for contaminating an apartment's water supply with a potentially brain-destroying dose of LSD. Geoffrey Weston and John Taylor, the intended victims, weren't available for comment, but Lieutenant Holder, who heads up the investigation, discounted rumors that police brutality played any part in the woman's death. According to Holder, "she just gasped and dropped dead. There wasn't a thing we could do. CPR was totally ineffective."

Senator Throckingham, whose office employed the suspect, confirmed that the woman had a history of arteriosclerosis and had recently undergone catheterization of an affected artery. At the same time he decried the police tactic of conducting late-night grillings. According to the Senator, Amy Sheldon was a quiet, dependable worker and he found it "difficult to believe that she could be involved in anything as despicable as a poisoning." Ted Sheldon, her estranged husband, reacted even more strongly and threatens a suit for false arrest and brutality against the Metropolitan Police Department.

I dropped the newspaper back onto the table.

"So that's how they would have handled us if we'd followed Sheldon. No wonder she drove off so quickly."

"Indeed," Geoff agreed. "We would have gotten a face full

114

of knockout gas while in hot pursuit at sixty miles per hour. They were still trying for a deadly accident. If, on the other hand, we'd drunk some water, it would have just been another case of foreigners overdosing on drugs. Some wag would have brought up my great uncle's unfortunate habit and lamented the family weakness."

"I suppose you're right." I stepped over to the stove and poured a cup of tea. "It's nice to finally have a bit of help with the investigation, though. The authorities seem to be falling all over each other in their efforts."

"Falling all over is about the size of it," Geoff commented. "The lieutenant should have put Amy Sheldon under surveillance instead of going against my advice by arresting her. She might have led us directly to the mastermind. But no, Holder had to demonstrate his independence by botching everything. Now we're left with trying to track down the invisible someone who rented the shoe store totally through the mails and employed a postal drop to do even that. I've been in touch with the real estate people.

"What else is new? Oh yes. About an hour ago another minion of the law called, identified himself as FBI Agent Pollard and demanded we turn every scrap of evidence we have over to him, including that pile of shoes out there. I told him we had no evidence until we proved it was evidence and that he'd better bring a court order and a ton of personal identification with him. Then I called the regional office to see if Pollard was Pollard. He was. We desperately need cooperation with the authorities, but I'm afraid we'll have to settle for competition. I rang up Throckingham to see if he could apply some influence. Status with the FBI and locals as official consultants would be an immense help." As he talked Geoff pried loose a center section of heel from a shoe he was working on and uncovered a hard plastic shell underneath.

"Do you think it's wise to deal through Throckingham?" I said, sipping tentatively at my tea to test its temperature. "After all, he was Amy Sheldon's boss. In my opinion that makes him a prime suspect."

"Yes," Geoff remarked, "I guess it does, though I doubt our murderer's doltish enough to be so obvious. Suspect or not, Throckingham's been more than cooperative. If you look on the sofa you'll find a pouch containing virtually everything we requested of him. We've had a regular parade of special messengers drop by this morning."

Setting aside my cup, I strolled to the living room for a look see, at least at Throckingham's data. I fumbled with the envelope's shoestring fastener and slid out a packet of 8" x 10" aerial glossies plus dossiers on a regular Who's Who of public figures. Each photo evidently employed a new top secret technique for spying through cloud layers because Washington's familiar street pattern was clearly recognizable though slightly hazy. The exact time to the thousandth of a second was superimposed on the upper right hand corner of every shot. As I flipped from picture to picture I could clearly see lightning bolts strike both the Library of Congress grounds and the Bethesda Chevy Chase Country Club. We now had visual evidence that there hadn't been a laser gun or super Tazer involved.

The dossiers proved equally interesting. Throckingham had gone beyond the mere list of Strong campaign supporters we'd requested and had included a biographical sketch of each.

Harrison Dodd of Dodd Chemical appeared to be one of the prime bankrollers for the effort. At fifty-five he was described as vigorous, a near genius, and a doctrinaire conservative. His support required the future candidate, however, to take a moderate position on environmental waste disposal.

Desmond Billings was serving his fourth term in the Senate and was a man with almost the political clout of Throckingham himself. He wasn't, however, considered a suitable presidential candidate since an operation for a brain tumor several years ago had left his left leg paralyzed, weakened the other and had confined him to a wheelchair with occasional forays on crutches. He *was* considered

116

suitable for the largely ceremonial post of President *pro tempore* of the Senate, which office he held with distinction. The fellow had managed reelection in his home state, but didn't have the vigor for national campaigning.

I wondered how Throckingham would have assessed FDR's chances a few generations back.

Billings had gone through two philosophical flip flops at opportune moments during his career and wasn't altogether trusted by the right wing of his party though he currently professed agreement with their views and possessed a photographic memory which came in handy during campaigning.

Carl Johnson was, at thirty-eight, considered a comer in party circles. He'd already served three terms in the House and was a definite prospect for higher office.

Jacob Manville was probably the most likely individual to follow in Strong's footsteps. He was tall and strikingly handsome, which was considered a definite asset. The man also had a knack for not sticking his foot in his mouth. He had had foreign service experience as ambassador to Yugoslavia and had directed the FBI during a previous administration before running successfully for the Senate. I could just imagine Throckingham calling him to smooth our relationship with the federal police.

Lillian Billings was the only woman in the group but appeared in some respects to outshine the others. She'd served as a trade representative to the Soviet Union, as undersecretary for Urban Affairs, and had for years directed International Bionics and Aerospace, one of the high tech conglomerates currently on the leading edge of research and development. She was anything but a rubber stamp for her husband Desmond.

The sixth and the last of the kingmakers was Lonnie Carlyle whose family made it a habit of electing each generation's sons into high and prestigious offices. They specialized in blue blood and green cash and had all but lived down the source of their fortune. Lonnie appeared to be a decent and rather charming chap but thoroughly out of his league when grouped with the political heavyweights mentioned on the other pages. At twenty-seven he was . . . .

"John!" Weston's excited voice jolted me from my studies. "Come have a look at something quite remarkable!"

As I glanced up I noticed that Geoff had pried some miniature electronic device from its teflon heel shell and was giving it a quick once-over through his magnifier. I hurried to the counter for a ringside view. The apparatus, whatever it was, proved to be the most compact unit imaginable since fully half its space was taken up with a battery and some kind of transformer, which left little room for the array of microchips huddled together in honeycomb fashion without even the luxury of a circuit board.

"It looks," Geoff volunteered, "rather like some of the current satellite innards, doesn't it? No added weight. No wasted space. But you'll notice that every chip is available on the open market. This thing was built so it couldn't be traced. What do you make of the device?"

"Well," I hazarded, "from the switch on top, it's obviously activated by pressure when the foot's laced into the shoe. And . . . the general appearance reminds me somewhat of an electronic flash gun. There's a battery and a high frequency transformer for building up a charge. For the life of me, though, I can't make heads nor tails of the rest of it."

Geoff placed his magnifying glass down next to the gadget.

"You will in just a few moments," he promised. "You'd best stash all but one pair of the shoes in the wardrobe. This place should start filling up rather soon. It's amazing what advertising one's phone number on the tele can do. We must have fully three hundred pairs of shoes in that stack. Half of Capitol Hill's probably walking around barefoot."

"That," I responded, while savoring the image he'd conjured up, "almost calls for a visit to the Senate gallery. The homespun humor should fairly gush from the podium today."

"Shouldn't it, though. Normally pedantic men . . . . "

The telephone jangled insistently and Geoff stepped over

had been, he would have surely gagged.

"You've got to be kidding! You guys are unreal. Maybe I should stay with you and . . . . "

"No thanks," Geoff cut him off. "I'm wearing a microphone tie clasp and so is John." He pulled what looked like a transistor radio earphone from his jacket pocket and stuck it in his ear as Pollard watched through the mirror. "If I see anything suspicious I'll let John know so we can act in unison. If he sees a threat, all he has to do is say 'duck.' We'll be covering each other from a distance. What's more, if there is an attack, it will occur because I announced to Congress and the Fleet Streeters where I was going not because of Miss Guerrero. The uncertainty of when the lightning would strike, you'll remember, removes her and her father from suspicion."

"Maybe in your book," Pollard rejoined, "but not in mine. We're protecting Congress because the murderer probably has back-up plans. He or *she* may have had them for Kidd and Strong, too, if they didn't croak before the crucial vote."

"What a quaint vocabulary you have," Weston observed blandly. "It hides your college degree nicely, I must say."

"Nuts!"

Pollard broke off the conversation and stared straight ahead at the road. After a few moments, the silence became oppressive. I attempted to re-establish communication.

"You know, Clyde," I pointed out, "we probably won't have any trouble at all. The murderer knows how careful we've been to hide our itinerary until now. He has to be suspicious of Geoff's public announcement. It sounded too much like baiting a trap. Although Geoff hasn't said so, I believe he intended it to sound that way so the killer would sit on his hands for awhile."

"That, at least, makes some sense," the agent conceded. "But if there is trouble, you're probably both dead meat. Don't aim at the arm. Shoot for the scuzball's heart."

I shook my head. "It's not my job to kill. Christ died for

129

that man just as much as for you and me. The beggar may not have heard the gospel and I'd hate to see him die without at least having a listen. I say, Clyde, have you ever heard the good news? There's someone out there somewhere who may someday blow a hole in your own heart."

I awaited a response from the front seat, but it didn't come.

"Everyone of us," I continued, in hopes he was paying attention, "stands condemned before God the Father not just for a few 'little' sins but for a corrupt 'thoughtstyle' rooted in our nature. We play mind games to put the best face on selfishness, pride and sensuality, but all the cosmetics in the world can't hide from Him who we really are. He sits as judge and declares 'Unfit for heaven. Unholy. Accursed. Imperfect. About to be sentenced to hell.'

"The Defense Attorney turns to each of us and says, 'Entrust your life to me and I'll get you off. I already died for all those sins to make a free pardon available to you. Trust me enough to retain me and depend upon me. Stop clinging to those mental addictions and accept me. Like Perry Mason, I've never lost a case.'

"I retained that Attorney a few years back by giving up on myself, asking Him for clemency, and accepting Him as my Savior. That very instant I was pardoned. His Spirit also started making changes inside me in the way I thought and reacted. He not only got me off, He's been rehabilitating me ever since."

Agent Pollard sat stone-faced in the front seat. I couldn't tell if he was ignoring us or simply considering the import of what I'd said. By now we were driving through the park-like mall that extended from the Capitol to the Washington Monument and beyond. Huge buildings in the Smithsonian complex formed rows on both sides of us.

"Your eloquence," Geoff finally said, addressing our companion, "will be just as profuse if you ever approach the Judge alone and have to argue your own case. You really should pay attention to what John's been saying."

Pollard took a deep breath and blew it out in annoyance. "I make it a point never to talk about politics or religion. Nobody ever wins those arguments. They just cause bad feelings."

"On whose part?" Weston wondered aloud. "Yours or the others? I assure you that our hides are rather thick. Furthermore, I fail to see that conversation's only legitimate goal is conquest. Whatever happened to 'comprehension,' 'inspiration,' and 'reassessment?' I pity you, Pollard. There's very little worthwhile that you can discuss after subtracting religion and politics. Both impinge on science, the arts, relief efforts, education, mass media, economics. Religion and politics aren't two little compartments that you can neatly shut off and forget. They encompass the totality of what it means to be human. Even communists can't get away from the duo. They just make politics their religion."

Clyde steered the motorcar over to a yellow painted curb and hit the brakes. "Can it, Weston. You're not conning me into your discussion. Besides, we're here."

Geoff favored him with a smile. "The Christian Scientist would, of course, dispute that point since he denies the reality of 'here' and the physical nature of 'we.' The existentialist would be concerned with the subjective feelings of 'we.' The Buddhist would question which sphere . . . . "

Weston ducked as a well directed styrofoam cup sailed past his right ear and out the window. Then he laughed.

"Ah, Clyde, there's hope for you yet. You've at least progressed to pantomime. I'll gladly 'can it' and open the container another day. Meanwhile, when you get time, be a good chap and give Inspector Robledo a jingle down in Mexico City. Have him investigate Gabriel Delgado Soto, his father Ricardo, and their Comodo Shoe Company. I'm particularly interested in their economic status, *political* leanings, and the firm's exports to the U.S. The few dozen ready-mades in our shoe pile don't show a brand name. Have Robledo check for generic manufacturing, lean hard on Soto, and put the whole clan under protective surveillance. I also

131

need a report from Twigg of Scotland Yard on the status of his interrogation. Oh yes, and one last thing . . . pull some strings to have the coroner send me whatever catheter he finds in Amy Sheldon's body. If she just underwent a balloon-type cleaning, that's one thing; but if there was any arterial implant, I want it."

"But I don't see . . . . "

"Precisely." Geoff leaned over and patted him on the shoulder. "You've avoided too many interesting conversations. You don't see because your field of vision's too narrow. I don't like coincidences. When potential witnesses die under questioning, that makes me suspicious. When I hear of previous operations, I become curious. Did anyone ever tell you there's a *religious* science fiction book in which the villain installs 'heart plugs' in his vassels so he can bleed them to death at his slightest displeasure? Does that give you any ideas? I want that catheter!"

Pollard's knitted brows clearly showed his reservations. "I'll do my best," he responded dubiously, "but the coroner's going to think I've got a screw loose."

The staircase was as wide as a boulevard and the pillared porch looked like the entrance to some temple on the Acropolis. Weston, however, didn't stop to admire the grandeur. He was, in fact, taking the steps two at a time, and I found myself falling behind despite my best efforts to the contrary. The studded leather doors, in fact, closed behind him before I could quite reach them. I heard his voice tinnily in my earphone.

"Don't worry, John. There isn't a billy in sight. It's better that we enter separately and keep our distance. I'm turning left to the alcove with the information table in it. She's supposed to be waiting there . . . . I've spotted one Secret Service man. They must be pulling double shifts what with the crunch. He's one of the gentlemen from last night. There don't seem to be any others."

I pried open the door and stepped inside to encounter one

of the most aesthetically pleasing and at the same time disquieting chambers I could have imagined. Massive black marble pillars the size of redwood trunks supported a central dome under which a marble fountain gushed forth merrily. Wide side corridors lined with flowing-robed statues offered entrance to the exhibit rooms.

"Beautiful," I commented to Geoff, "but deadly. I doubt I can cover all those columns. They offer perfect concealment for an assassin. I'll be glad when the two of you have moved into the galleries."

"You and me both," Weston confessed.

I caught sight of Paloma standing by the doughnut-shaped information table. She seemed a natural part of the gallery with that flowing black hair of hers, although she was much too thin at the waist to have appealed to artists of an earlier age. She hadn't seen either of us, though, because her attention was fixed on a painting. Paloma was, in fact, gazing at the exhibit with such studious intensity that my partner had to touch her on the shoulder for attention. Then she jumped.

"Oh, Geoff, it's you! You shouldn't sneak up on me like that."

"Sorry," Weston responded with a grin, "but when I asked the Light Brigade to charge ahead of me as a warning, they said they'd been rejected by American Express. When I asked General Patton to let loose a volley, he said 'tanks but no tanks.' So I opted to tap your shoulder, for which indiscretion I shall be fed to hungry crocodiles in the morning."

Paloma responded with a pleasant laugh that all but drowned out my own groan. She must, indeed, have been studying our language, though I almost hoped she'd misinterpreted.

"I was a little *preocupado*," she admitted, "but, *mi querido*, it's such an exquisite painting, don't you think? I drink it in and the more I look the more there is to see."

Geoff gazed first at the animated sparkle in her eyes, then over at the wall. The elaborately framed oil was so large that I could make out most details even from my vantage point. I recognized it at once as Salvador Dali's "Last Supper."

"It is interesting," my partner agreed after a moment. "But Shaffner's critique has rather spoiled it for me. He believed Dali, by painting Christ translucent, made an existential attack on the historical nature of Jesus."

Paloma studied the work of art a moment longer.

"I know that Shaffner is a great philosopher," she concluded, "but I do not believe he understood the painting. Look at the drinking glass before Jesus. It's modern. This is a special occasion but it can't be the one in Palestine two thousand years ago. It just can't!"

"Hmm . . . " Weston considered the matter further, then plucked a gallery brochure from the counter and skimmed it.

"You would," he conceded at last, "appear to be right. The craggy scene out the window isn't Galilee at all but the Bay of Port Lligat as the painter would have seen it from his own window. That would tend to date events in the twentieth century, wouldn't it? According to the leaflet, Dali also returned in old age 'to Christianity and traditional values.' He seems, in fact, to be as much a mirror image in early and late life as his painted characters. The agnostic embraced Christianity—at least as he understood it. Thank you."

"For what?"

"For giving me renewed appreciation for a magnificent work of art."

"You're welcome, kind sir."

He offered her his hand and she readily responded.

"It's funny," Weston reflected as they walked hand in hand to the next painting, "how fuzzy the time element *can* be. Take us, for example. We've only known each other for two years, and most of that time we've had to be content with letters. Yet I feel I've known you a much longer time. Perhaps that's because it's easier to open up and express feelings and aspirations on a sheet of paper than face to face."

Paloma's eyes sparkled as she looked up at him. "It seems long to me, too, *mi corazon*. But then I've been praying for you for nearly ten years. At least I think I may have been."

"Ten years?"

"*Sí.* When I was still in secondary school, I started praying, although I did not know your name or who you were. Now and then I even sensed danger and woke up in the night to ask God's protection for you. You think I'm silly, don't you?"

"No," Geoff gazed at her soberly. "Sometimes I've wondered at God's intervention when prayer was the farthest thing from my mind. When was the last time you felt that urgent need?"

She didn't hesitate. "Early Wednesday morning when I woke up. Did anything unusual happen?"

Geoff bit his lip. "Figuring time differences," he calculated, "I'd say most definitely. I rather think your prayers instigated a traffic accident."

"Oh my! I'm sorry. I didn't know."

"Don't be. It saved our lives. Tell me, though, why you started praying so long ago. I'm fairly bursting with curiosity."

The two of them barely glanced at the next painting in line. As though by mutual consent, they started strolling toward the alcove entrance. I wished, though, that Geoff had chosen to hold hands with his left instead of his right. If the need arose, he would have to be a contortionist to reach his shoulder holster. I glanced nervously about, but couldn't detect anything suspicious. Tourists with cameras vied for space with disinterested school children herded here and there by well-intentioned teachers.

"My pastor," Paloma continued, "cautioned me back then to stop wondering if every boy I went out with was God's choice for me. I'd dated and prayed and broken up time after time. It began to seem God wasn't even listening. In reality I guess I was too possessive and frightened everyone away. Pastor Tomas told me God had to answer two sets of prayers, mine and the boy's, and He wasn't about to stick any Christian young man with me until I matured. The preacher advised me to expand my horizons so I would be a more interesting person, pray for my own spiritual and intellec-

135

tual growth, pray the same for that anonymous man in my future, and trust God to bring us together when we were ready and wouldn't be a temptation to each other. I've been following that advice ever since."

Even at a distance I could see her face redden into a very pretty blush as comprehension dawned concerning the implications of what she'd said.

"Oh my! What have I done? I've practically . . . . Ten years later and I still haven't learned my lesson. Will you forgive me for being unbelievably forward? I was just thinking of what happened, not of how it would sound to you."

"I quite understand." Weston began guiding her toward an area considerably removed from the main room's central fountain and off the beaten tourist trail. "Let's step over there a moment where we can speak a tad more privately. I have something to say to you which is for your ears only."

I suspected that that last comment might be for my benefit, but I was not about to shut down the receiver, particularly with my friend headed for the most secluded and, therefore, potentially most dangerous spot under the dome. Out of the corner of my eye I could see the gray-flanneled Secret Service man hurrying as unobtrusively as possible for a better position. I began drifting that way myself, but at a more leisurely pace.

Paloma's blush had faded and she allowed Geoff to guide her forward in her confusion. She looked for all the world like some schoolgirl approaching the fireplace on Christmas morning without knowing quite what to expect but excited by the very mystery. Only in this case it was a pillar, not a fireplace that loomed ahead.

"What is this deep, dark secret?" she coaxed.

"You'll see soon enough."

Before I could react, the two disappeared behind the column.

"You are," Geoff observed very seriously but in almost a whisper, "my friend forever and, therefore, the most cherished of treasures. I want you to know how much I

136

admire your honest openness. Don't ever lose it. You're also breathtakingly, stunningly beautiful."

There was a second's silence followed by rustling and then a strange, rhythmic double thump that repeated itself like the ticking of a watch. Alarmed, I started quickly in their direction but then pulled up as it finally occurred to me what had happened. I was hearing the sound of two hearts pressed against each other and beating almost in unison. A moment later the thumping stopped and I could just barely make out Paloma's answer.

"*Ay que,* Geoffrey. But you express your feelings very well indeed face to face." I switched off the receiver and ambled over to strike up a conversation with the Secret Service man. My partner might be in danger, but it was not of a sort about which I could do anything.

11
CAN AMERICA SURVIVE?

Rock Creek Park was aptly named. As we drove along the narrow road hugging the banks of the meandering stream, we could see that the local landmark was literally strewn with granite. Giant oaks and pines obscured the afternoon sun except for occasional twinkles that managed to filter through.

"Let's be grateful for small favors," Weston remarked as he drove. "It was a bit of all right to get the motorcar back so quickly from the impound yard. That new alarm system the federals installed sounds like a regular Scottish banshee, doesn't it?"

"Try air raid siren," I quipped. "As I remember, folklore banshees howl to announce impending death. Speaking of death, I'm glad and rather surprised we survived that taxi drive to the FBI's yard. What possessed the locals to ship the Cadillac over to them anyway? That FBI regional office is in the scariest neighborhood I think I've ever entered. You know you're in trouble when you pull up to a stop sign and see empty-eyed addicts sitting on the porch steps of boarded up buildings whiling away the hours whittling blow gun darts with switchblades."

Geoff chuckled. "That is," he assessed, "a slight exaggeration. I admit, though, that the spot could have been more convivial."

"More convivial! There's a polluted river on one side and a slum on the other. That's like referring to Devil's Island as 'a tad bit understated'."

"All right. Have it your way." He raised both hands momentarily from the wheel in a gesture of acquiescence.

"We deserve combat pay and an extra ration of chocolate."

I shuddered. "No chocolate for me, thanks. Pollard got under my skin with that remark about me being fat. I'm afraid he hit rather too near the mark."

"Bosh and balderdash!" Weston opined. "The trouble with society today is that we don't allow for individual differences and try to shove everyone into a mold. You saw the paintings at the National Gallery. Tele exercise leaders would have had three quarters of those models on the mat doing aerobics to the bounce and wail of harpsichord Dixieland. And I've never yet seen an evangelical self-help book entitled *Free to be Plump*. We're not free to be plump because everyone's been drumming it into our heads for years that 'thin is in.' Oh certainly, gross overweight has been proven harmful, but there's a lot more leeway than we think. A woman who's ten or fifteen pounds over what she considers ideal often suffers the consequences of a poor self-image. You're a little beyond that, but the dieting goal isn't so far away, is it?"

"No," I reflected, "I guess not when you put it that way."

"Remember, too," Geoff encouraged, "that you're not necessarily a glutton for being overweight. You've been underactive this winter, not an overeater."

"Thank you," I responded. "You've put the whole matter in a much more encouraging perspective."

"Don't mention it." Geoff craned his neck and slowed as we drove by a two-story red brick structure clinging to a slope. "That must be Billings' house. We left the park proper a block back when we hit West Beach Drive. Funny a man in a wheelchair would choose to live on such a hill. It is a beautiful section, though. I guess he moved here before the paralysis and grew too fond of the place to leave."

"I think I would myself," I agreed. "He may go on a roller coaster ride when he comes out the door, but he certainly has the world at his fingertips when he's indoors. Look at that ham antenna up the bank. It's a beauty. Why don't you park on the next cross street and we can walk back. I need to get in some exercise."

Weston, who was forced by 'no parking' signs to take my advice, finally found a spot, angled the front wheels to grab the curb and set the emergency brake. A few moments later we were standing on a neatly terraced area confronting a porch sporting both steps and a circular wheelchair ramp which reminded me rather of a flat noodle twisted to the shape of a corkscrew. The senator was quite evidently determined to enjoy his yard even if he had to cement over and ramp up half of it in the process. I admired his gumption.

We'd hardly started up the stairs when a loud bell rang inside and a butler hastened to open the screen door. I looked behind me and noticed photoelectric units clamped to opposing railing posts. Their twins graced the ramp. This was one house, I mused, which wouldn't have pets or the servants would be run ragged. The system would work wonderfully, though, if one were staggering home under a load of packages. We were ushered into a living room which ran the width of the very ample home and displayed floor to ceiling bookshelves on every wall.

Desmond Billings, thick-browed and barrel-chested, wheeled out from behind a walnut desk in the far left corner and impelled himself by deft wrist movements in our direction.

He had a hearty voice. "Glad to see you gentlemen. I'm sorry we couldn't meet downtown, but I took off a little early. I hope you'll excuse an old man for his aches and pains."

"Not at all," I responded sincerely. I felt a bit of pain myself as his vice-like grip left me flexing my right hand.

"It's so good," he enthused, "to finally speak with you one on one, or should I say one on two. I'm an avid fan of yours. Say, that case where you uncovered Arthur Heath's shenanigans at the Pinehurst Laboratories was really a gem. It's about time scientists discovered there are forbidden zones to research. Some of the Pentagon generals should learn that lesson. You have no idea what bizarre funding requests get shoved our way from time to time."

"I'm sure I haven't," Weston agreed. "The list wouldn't happen to include lightning attracting shoes, would it?"

Billings's smile disappeared. "Don't I wish. Then we'd have the mental pervert whose been squashing people like cockroaches." He suddenly closed his eyes and gritted his teeth in pain. "Excuse me," he finally managed, "I still get these twinges. You've heard of people who have legs amputated but still feel them? It's the same kind of thing. One of my legs has been useless for years, but sometimes it feels like the other one would if I let it go to sleep, then dropped a hot iron on it."

I shuddered at the thought. "You have my sympathy," I assured him. "I think I'd die, personally, before letting anyone start sawing holes in my skull."

He ruefully ran his hand over the barely visible scar behind his left ear.

"In my case," he commented, "I'd be dead even with the operation except for the new leucogen blood treatment. The tumor was cancerous."

"I'm sorry."

"Oh, don't be. They got all of it." He snapped his fingers. "Like that! Now tell me what it is you two need to know. I realize you're busy with the investigation and probably don't have even a minute to waste."

I glanced significantly at Geoff, but suppressed the impulse to bring up a certain art gallery.

"First off," my partner began, "it would be of some help to discover why the murderer singled you out for a pair of shoes."

Billings gripped the arms of the chair so hard his knuckles turned white.

"I'd like to know that myself. It's enough I wear braces, hobble a few steps each day on crutches and roll around the rest of the time in this. If lightning struck in a crowd, it'd probably zero in on me anyway because of all the metal I lug

141

around. I don't need some joker turning me into a lightning rod."

"Nor do any of us," Geoff agreed. "Would you say there was anything unusual about the group that assembled this morning to see the demonstration?"

"No. They were of every political stripe. Both parties were fairly well represented." He drummed his fingers on the chair arm. "There was one thing, but it's probably not important."

"Let me be the judge of that," Geoff prodded.

Billings eyed us both shrewdly. "Don't quote me on this, now. The only political hack in the bunch was Throckingham. Please don't take it as a boast on my part, but I'd say the murderer was bent on eliminating quality statesmen."

"You and Throckingham," I reminded him, "were working together to promote Strong's presidential bid."

"Yes." Desmond acknowledged, "and I'd have worked with the devil himself if it could have gotten Strong elected. Throckingham has plenty of favors stored up to cash in on, so he was useful. He is also boring, not very trustworthy, and unimaginative. He's the kind of man the Nazis would have selected as resident quisling when they occupied a town."

Geoff extracted a half-empty bag of peanuts from his jacket pocket and popped a few into his mouth.

"You say," he managed around the nuts, "that you'd have worked with the devil. That's a pretty radical statement. Why were you, if you'll excuse the pun, so strongly for Strong?"

"Because," Billings asserted, "Strong or whoever takes up his banner may be the last hope for the Western democracies."

"How so?"

The Senator gestured toward a row of shelving by the side window. "The books over there," he informed us, "trace the spread of communism from the 1940s to the present. The advance, my friend, has been inexorable because the com-

142

munists have a system to which they're totally dedicated, at least insofar as government policy is concerned. We, on the other hand, aren't quite sure what we believe. We've spiked capitalism with such a liberal dose of socialistic tomfoolery that we've run out of idealogy to export. The result is that we're currently losing a square mile of territory every one point three seven days. You don't have to be a genius to figure out what that means. We will inevitably be overrun unless we re-establish a purer form of capitalism and export it as avidly as the communists do. I believe Strong's election would have revitalized capitalism in the United States."

Weston studied him quizzically. "And the export process?"

"Oh," Desmond shrugged off the question, "that would have come a good bit later. Isn't it absolutely silly, gentlemen, that we spend so much time and money perfecting a defense system to make a nuclear strike impossible for either side, when the missile button is the only thing currently saving us from invasion by enemies who have ten point seven three times the western world's combined conventional fire power?"

"That," Geoff responded, "is, of course, debatable since it doesn't consider theatre nuclear weapons or our technological superiority."

"Which," Billings countered, "wouldn't be worth a hill of beans against guerilla warfare tactics if the enemy chose its conventional approach. How many communist moles do you think there are among all those millions of illegal immigrants we've let sneak in during the last few years? We're afraid to bring that up, of course, for fear of losing the Hispanic vote. But if I were dictator of Cuba or Nicaragua, I'd have smuggled in a good sized army of saboteurs by now. I assume that's just what they've done."

"So," I inquired, "what can any one individual do? You make the future sound rather grim."

"It is," he acknowledged. "As for myself, I'll continue working for whoever takes Strong's place. If that fails . . . well, I've hollowed out a bomb shelter in the hill behind us. I hope I never have to use it." He gestured broadly. "The survival of our liberty to discuss and imagine, gentlemen, depends on the survival of this nation under a capitalistic system."

"That sounds," Geoff noted, "awfully like the climax of a speech." He popped the remainder of the nuts into his mouth, crinkled the bag and returned it to his pocket. "Since you're not in a position to dismiss us by standing, I'll take it as the verbal equivalent. It's been a pleasure to make your acquaintance, though I hope you're wrong about the gravity of the situation."

The Senator took the lead, wheeling briskly toward the front door. "So do I, Mr. Weston. So do I."

A few moments later, when I backed the car down onto West Beach Drive and began retracing our route toward town, Billings favored us with a friendly wave from the porch.

By now government offices were shutting down for the weekend so the number of politicians we could interview had shrunk drastically. We elected not to crisscross Washington in some quixotic search for scattered bureaucrats but to return home and see if Pollard had dropped off any goodies. It had already been a full day. I switched on an all-news station and we relied on the resident traffic reporter's sage advice to steer us clear of the worst automotive log jams.

12
OPERATION FRUIT BASKET

Two American equivalents to bobbies still stood guard at the entrance to our apartment house. Evidently the locals were not nearly so overtaxed by the workload we'd piled on them as were the federals. It came as a disappointment, but not particularly as a surprise, when one of the patrolmen volunteered the information that we'd had no visitors during our absence. I suppose it was too much to expect that Clyde could have unearthed as much dirt as we'd requested in so short a time. Geoff led the way to our apartment, turned the key in the lock, stepped aside, and nudged the door open with the barrel of his revolver. The living room was just as we'd left it, strewn with papers and cigarette butts and with half the furniture piled along the left wall. Hotel maids, I concluded, must really hate political conventions.

"Well," Geoff concluded as he stepped over the thresshold, "no one appears to have broken in."

"Who'd want to," I groused. "Breaking out's a much more attractive prospect. I'll get to work with a broom while you check out the other rooms."

"Righto." Geoff slammed the door and began creeping very carefully down the hall.

About the time he disappeared into the bathroom, the raucous jangle of the telephone nearly sent me into cardiac arrest. I followed the cord to the pile of furniture and dug out the phone from under an end table.

"Sleuths Ltd., Taylor speaking. May I help you?"

The voice at the other end of the line radiated confidence. "You certainly may. This is Senator Manville. Would it be all right if I came over with some close friends in,

145

say, half an hour? We have some rather urgent business to discuss."

I calculated the clean-up time. "That should work out just fine, Senator. We'll let the guards out front know you're expected."

"Thank you very much."

"Don't mention it. Cheerio."

I recradled the receiver and made a mad dash for the kitchen broom closet.

"Geoff," I called down the hall, "make a quick job of that search. We've got high-powered visitors on their way here. I'll need a hand with the debris in the living room."

I heard a sliding door rumble as my partner checked one of the bedroom wardrobes.

"Be right there. I've got one more room to search. Then it won't take more than a minute to change into my tux."

"Into your tux! Whatever for?"

I banged the closet closed and started sweeping my way back to the meeting area.

"For the play, of course," Weston declared. "The curtain rises at eight. I hope you don't mind awfully not going. There's a frightful lot of work that's still got to be done here."

I picked up the pace of my sweeping, choosing to take out my frustration on the oak flooring and linoleum rather than on my friend. I'd assumed the gallery tour had taken that insufferable play's place.

"Congratulations," I projected toward the bedroom, "on your recovery from workaholism. Don't you think, though, you wasted enough time already this afternoon?"

My partner's reply echoed jovially down the hall.

"Wasted! I'll have you know, good fellow, that the Smithsonian trip was an essential part of the investigation."

"Nice work if you can get it," I noted tongue-in-cheek. "I marvel at your relentless, if somewhat unorthodox, interrogation."

Weston laughed. "Interrogation wasn't my purpose, as you well know. Mark my words, though. That meeting's going to

146

produce some unexpected results."

"It already has," I informed him. "I got to talk with Paloma's bodyguard during the event and found out he thinks you're acting fully as nutty as I do."

"The nut," my partner responded, "is one of nature's wonders. It's sturdy, exquisitely crafted and full of surprises."

Dust billowed up around me and sent me into a fit of coughing.

When the knock came this time, the sofa had so recently been raced across the room to its customary spot that I could imagine it breathing hard. All the furnishings, however, appeared as though they had rested in stolid permanence for months. I tossed the dustcloth under a seat cushion and Geoff and I stepped over to greet our guests.

As it turned out, the doorway framed a delegation of three. Carl Johnson I recognized from the help he'd given Geoff during the lightning demonstration. He stood a little over six feet tall and looked more like a quarterback turned sportscaster than a congressman. There was little question as to the second gentleman's occupation since his uniform pronounced him a U.S. Army colonel. I'd never seen him before. By process of elimination, the tall grey-haired gentleman in front with his hand out had to be Senator Manville. I reached over and pumped that hand vigorously.

"Glad to meet you, Senator. I'm afraid I didn't recognize you this morning or I would have had a word with you. Do come in."

Manville smiled, revealing perfect teeth that went well with his firm jaw. He definitely looked "presidential" and would be a formidable campaigner.

"One word," he quipped as he stepped forward, "is about all you would have gotten in that melee. I'd like you to meet two close friends of mine. The one you know." He gestured toward Johnson. "We found out this morning Carl isn't much of a conductor, but he's an excellent legislator."

The congressman closed the door behind him and shook

hands all around. His voice was deep and as distinguished as a radio announcer's. "It's an honor to meet you, gentlemen. All of Capitol Hill's in your debt."

"I hope so," Weston half joked. "Before we're through, I may have to call in a few IOUs to capture the killer."

"You name it," Johnson responded sincerely. "Many's the time I've been grateful I wasn't in somebody else's shoes. Today I was glad I wasn't in my own."

"And the colonel over here," Manville broke in, "is Harry Claypool. He may be the Pentagon's resident tennis pro. At least he runs me half to death whenever we play. He's also Chief of Army Intelligence, which is why we're here."

Weston steered the trio to the sofa. "Please be seated, gentlemen, and we'll get right down to cases."

They settled in and Geoff took his customary place on an easy chair opposite them. I started to follow suit but had a sudden inspiration.

"If you'll excuse me," I observed, "there's one matter which should be attended to before anyone says anything."

I pulled the bug detector from my pocket, switched it on, and started aiming around the room. Almost immediately it responded with a loud beeping which raised in pitch as I directed it toward my partner's general location. Visibly startled, he came quickly to his feet and stepped forward for my electronic inspection. The sounds, however, didn't seem at all affected by his presence. I next made passes over the chair with the same negative results. The floor lamp to the chair's left was, however, a different matter. Beeps became staccato and melted into a high pitched squeal as my arm descended from the shade to a book platform about a meter from the floor. I draped my hand with a handkerchief so as not to disturb fingerprints and pried the self-sticking transmitter from the platform's underside.

"Nasty critters," I commented as I disarmed it and slid it into my pocket. "Remarkably prolific, too! This must be the season for them."

"Indeed," Geoff commented as he eased back into his

chair. "Be a good chap and make sure it hasn't had babies."

I made a 360° sweep of the room without arousing my electronic bloodhound to any further frenzies. Meanwhile our guests seemed to take my warning literally and looked uneasily about the room in total silence.

"Gentlemen," Weston said, "our conversation is now quite private. Let's get on with it."

Colonel Claypool belatedly removed his hat, revealing a regulation haircut.

"Perhaps," he observed, "I should be the one to start. I hope you're right about the privacy because heads will roll if you're not—among them my own."

"I'm aware," Weston noted, "that you're one of the inside leaks Manville uses so he can better watchdog the military."

"Sources," the Senator replied. "I prefer that to 'leaks.' The man doesn't break security by reporting to me, I assure you, since I chair the Armed Services Subcommittee."

"True enough," Geoff agreed, "but John and I chair nothing. Go on. We're all ears."

Manville and Claypool glanced uncertainly at each other. Then Harry stifled his reluctance.

"Mr. Weston," he charged verbally on, "you probably realize that this nation uses its embassies as bases for gathering information in certain unfriendly foreign capitals. What you may not know, however, is that we also sometimes find it necessary to gather intelligence from amongst our allies. If evidence of those activities ever got out it would . . . well, let me put it this way. A repairman once got lost in the Pentagon attic and fell through the ceiling into a joint chiefs' meeting. The consternation caused by his untimely entrance would be miniscule compared with that felt by my superiors if our spying on friendlies were ever proven."

"Skip the preliminaries," Weston directed. "You or the CIA or both have been spying on Mexico. What's the scoop?"

"Not only on Mexico," the Colonel corrected, "also, I'm afraid, on your own country."

Geoff eyed him bleakly. "Go on."

"Well, sir, we're beginning to see a disturbing pattern develop. This telephone number, for example, was found on the body of a suspected Irish Republican killed while breaking into your office." He passed a photographic print over to Weston who in turned handed it my way.

202-555-97-61

"We've determined," Claypool continued, "that the number belongs to a phone booth a few blocks from here. That would, of course, support your theory that there's a connection between events here and the Concorde bombing."

Weston nodded. "It does more than that," he observed. "It also establishes a possible link between the Irish Republicans and that attack on Paloma Guerrero and Gabriel Delgado Soto."

"Excuse me. I don't follow."

"Why, it's simplicity itself." Geoff folded his arms and leaned back. "Someone in this country ordered the break-in. The thief needed a number to call when the job was done so he could get final payment. The blighter who dictated the numbers to him was probably Mexican. Notice the last two sets, 97-61. An American would have written 9761. It's the custom in Mexico, however, to conclude with two hyphenated pairs. A few other countries, of course, follow that same practice, but I think it's safe to assume the man who did the hiring was Mexican."

The colonel received the photo back from me and re-studied it.

"That," he concluded, "merely brings the pattern into sharper focus. We've been getting reports from paid informants in Central America about something called 'Operation Fruit Basket.' They haven't come up with any details yet, but we suspect something big's about to happen. Then a few hours ago a hit squad tried to torch the Comodo Shoe Company and murder the owner's family. Thanks to your warning to Inspector Robledo, only the elder Soto was wounded, and two killers were taken alive. According to a somewhat angry telephone conversation between Robledo and the arresting officers, the detectives first on the scene seem to have extracted confessions through some unauthorized methods. Both would-be killers mentioned the term 'Operation Fruit Basket' as well as naming several key communist guerilla leaders as accomplices. It's all going to make a big splash in tomorrow's papers. You predicted that attack. What can you tell us about the operation?"

"Not a single thing," Weston confided, ". . . yet. I'm afraid John and I are still rather like Hansel and Gretel munching at the edges of the witch's house."

"We've got to know about that plan," the Senator said with a note of urgency. "That Mexican aid package comes out of committee this Monday. If there's a real risk to our southern neighbors, I've got to help ram it through."

"Satellite photos," Claypool added, "show unusual shipping activity between eastern bloc countries and both Nicaragua and Cuba, but every crate's labeled as medicine, food or agricultural tools. We can't prove a military build-up, although some vehicles off-loaded were probably camouflaged tanks."

Geoff stared from one to the other of them. "I repeat, gentlemen, that I do not as yet know the full scope or purpose of this activity. I do have a few suspicions. I'd prefer to keep them to myself, however, until they are supported by evidence. Let me, in turn, ask you a question. If I should guarantee to expose Strong's killer and unmask that operation before a joint session of Congress next Monday morning at, say, nine o'clock, could you arrange for such a session?"

The senator swallowed hard. He obviously realized the potential for political damage if Geoff should prove unable to back up his words.

"Yes," he concluded, "I believe that could be done. It would technically have to be a joint 'meeting' since only the President speaks at a joint 'session,' but there's no substantial difference." He glanced aside. "What do you think, Carl? Could we manage it?"

151

"We could pull enough strings," Representative Johnson concurred. "Are you sure such a drastic move is called for, though?"

"The deeper I dig into this case," Geoff mused, "the more I believe it is."

"Very well," Manville concluded as he rose to his feet, "you've got it. We'll contact the proper authorities tomorrow morning." He reached over and grasped my partner's hand. "I must say you didn't waste much time calling in your IOUs."

Geoff smiled warmly. "I've noticed, Senator, that vouchers tend to depreciate with age."

"They do," the statesman agreed, "for a fact."

We escorted our guests to the door, said our goodbyes, indulged in another round of handshakes, and watched the chaps disappear down the hall. When they were safely out of sight, I gave Weston a sidelong glance.

"Geoff," I breathed, "did you have to stick your neck out quite so far? We may be the only blokes to ever be made citizens and then deported all in the space of a single weekend."

"It goes with the territory," Geoff observed seriously. "Our assassin piled blunder onto blunder trying to kill us. That resulted in the intensity of the investigation now going on. He's come to realize he's been his own worst enemy. Now he's sitting back to study the situation like that American computer which was once programmed to play chess and learn from its own mistakes. As long as he does, he's unassailable. We've got to shake him up a bit."

"Well," I concluded, "thinking you're going to expose him before a joint meeting of Congress certainly should do that. He'll be after us with everything short of the neutron bomb."

"Yes," Weston chuckled good-naturedly. "Isn't it wonderful? I'll be leaving presently for my date. After all, there shouldn't be any danger tonight. While I'm gone, be a good chap and work your way through that mountain of shoes. I'll need an assessment of wear, examination for fingerprints in the heel cavity, and a multitester voltage reading on each battery. Correlate that with the date each shoe was purchased. Let's see . . . you'll also need to check the bug for prints. I wonder how the FBI's attempts to trace its twins to the manufacturer are going. If you find a print, pass it along to Pollard if he ever shows up. I'm beginning to despair of the man. We may have the case solved before we even know who all the intended victims are. Well, I'd best be running along."

Before I could think of a reasonable protest to lodge, he'd gone the way of our distinguished visitors. I stared down the empty hallway for a moment, then turned finally to re-enter our quarters.

"Lord," I whispered under my breath, "please keep that irascible, bull-headed, cocky partner of mine alive and safe. He's the roughest diamond imaginable, but he's yours."

13
FIRE FIGHT

It was Mark Hatfield who once said something to the effect that membership in Congress fostered a prima donna complex about as effectively as did starring at the Met. Congressmen, I presume, never stop to dissect their shoes and sniff the aroma of sweaty feet. If they did, they'd be cured very quickly of any illusions they might have as to their own grandeur. I, for my part, began to feel ill before tearing apart my first hundred pair. It was with considerable relief sometime later that I approached my last heel while seated under an open window. There were no fingerprints in the cavities just as there had been none on the bug. Every shoe had moderate wear. All the batteries registered within a quarter volt of one another, except, of course, for Johnson's shoes which Geoff had discharged during the demonstration. The exercise was, from my point of view at least, a complete waste of time. I entered the last figures in my log beside the shoe owner's name and closed up shop for the night. The only interesting aspect to the entire evening was that Throckingham's name wasn't on any shoe tag in the pile. He'd evidently come for the demonstration out of interest in the case rather than because he'd been in personal danger. That made sense. If he'd worn the shoes, he would have been fried alongside of Strong. The omission made me wonder, however, about Billings' theory that the murderer was out to dispose of the innovative talent in Congress. Throckingham, the only "hack" in the meeting, had been immune. It was his aide, I reflected, who had tried to kill us.

With considerable weariness I sank into my easy chair, switched on the table lamp beside it, and immersed myself in reading the New Testament. It was a considerable relief to set aside crime for awhile and think about "whatever is pure, whatever is lovely." I paused deep in Matthew to ponder one such confrontation where the self-serving Pharisees accused Jesus of being a glutton, drunkard and friend of sinners. As I considered the matter, my stomach reminded me that I hadn't eaten a bite since breakfast.

The fare in the refrigerator turned out to be rather basic since neither Geoff nor I had had time for any shopping other than a quick trip to the corner store. I scavenged a half-eaten jar of peanut butter and spread a glue-like sandwich that did at least curb the hunger twinges. I was about to pour a glass of water for my dessert when Pollard's unmistakable banging at the entrance signalled his arrival.

When I admitted him, the agent brushed past me carrying a large, and apparently heavy, cardboard box which he dropped unceremoniously on the kitchen table. The poor fellow looked almost as haggard as I felt.

"There's your paperwork," he declared brusquely. "I hope you choke on it. I've got half of Congress up in arms about my snooping. The rumor is I'm trying to put together another Hoover file so the President can blackmail passage of his favorite bills. Meanwhile you guys continue sopping up the glory."

I pried open the lid and began lifting out the contents.

"We really appreciate all your efforts," I said sincerely. "And as for the glory, Geoff and I may change from hero to goat by Monday, so don't feel bad about your own status."

"Yeah," Pollard responded, "I heard about that joint meeting jazz. So you're putting on a bluff. I kinda' wondered."

I couldn't hide my sudden concern. "You heard?"

"Sure. It's all over town."

I pounded my fist down on the table with the force of a gavel. "That tears it! Geoff's out at some play with Paloma, confident the news won't leak until morning."

"Well then," Clyde noted with finality, "he's just going to have to take care of himself. I put every extra man I had in a two block radius around this building the moment I heard the news, but that's the extent of it. I'm not going to roust ticket takers to track him down. If I did, it'd likely give the killers the clue they needed to find him."

I nodded silent agreement. "No, there's not much we can do but pray and wait." I looked down disgustedly at the array of papers scattered across the table. "I could sure use your help in wading through this mess."

To my complete surprise he appeared to consider the matter. "I can give you maybe half an hour. My wife made it clear this morning she expects me home before TV sign off. Anyway, I can't stay long. What do you want me to do?"

He took his seat on one side of the table while I settled down on the opposite side and tossed the now empty box into the corner.

"Let's divide the case histories roughly in half," I decided aloud. "You read through your set and let me know whenever you run into a non sequitur, anything which seems strange, illogical, suspicious or just useful as background. You jot down your comments and I'll scribble mine as a condensation for Geoff."

"Sounds reasonable," Pollard agreed. "Most of this material is pretty routine stuff. Even the London report isn't all that full of revelations. The surviving thug says he was just following orders, and the leader's conveniently dead. Twigg has rounded up an entire terrorist cell, though."

"Bully for him," I declared, "even if the leads don't jump the ocean."

I shuffled my half of the confusion into a neat stack and scanned pages for the next few moments.

"You're certainly right when you say 'routine,'" I concurred at last. "The most exciting news so far is that Congressman Shilling was suspended for a week during third grade for fighting in the schoolyard."

"I can top that," Clyde observed with a chuckle. "Old man

Billings' only perfect grammar school scores were in attendance and deportment. He nearly flunked until his father stuck him in a private academy up in New England. Maybe there's hope for me yet."

"Well," I observed, "Einstein didn't blossom until he was in preparatory school which is roughly equivalent to your junior high. I do think, though, that you'd be better off at your age concentrating on spiritual change rather than on getting a Ph.D."

Pollard scowled. "There you go again," he complained, "circling back to religion. All right, wise guy, I do have one 'spiritual' question that's been gnawing at me for awhile. See if you can answer it. My wife's Jewish. Explain to me how a loving God like all you Christians preach could send a Jew to hell just for thinking Jesus isn't the Messiah."

I started skimming the next dossier.

"My word," I considered aloud, "that is a toughie. You won't listen to me very objectively, will you, with so much personally at stake?"

"House speaker Jarvis," Clyde noted as he continued the search through his stacks, "received heavy mob contributions when he ran for alderman in the Big Apple about twenty years back. That could be significant. As to my objectivity, try me. Tell me how God's love squares with sending Jews to hell."

I glanced up from my work. "Why don't we reverse the question for a minute. Could a just God really let anyone into heaven without a Messiah?"

"Sure. Why not?"

"Because to do so would repudiate all of Judaism. Look at the book of Leviticus. It's filled with offering after offering, sacrifice after sacrifice. The shedding of blood was absolutely necessary in the Old Testament to make atonement for sins. Men constantly brought the unblemished of their flocks. There was a veritable river of blood flowing on behalf of the nation. When was the last time your wife sacrificed even a pigeon?"

Pollard shrugged. "Never that I know of. They don't do it that way now."

"There you have it. The flow of blood stopped roughly two millennia ago. The law doesn't create holiness. It merely condemns infractions. How does your wife ever hope to stand holy before God without those sacrifices? Meal offerings can't do it. According to the Old Testament, blood has to be shed. Israel has only two alternatives according to its own foundation document. It can either begin animal sacrifice again and write off two thousand years of faithful Jews who died without making a single sin offering, or it can discover the Messiah. In the end, it has to either re-interpret the Old Testament to the point of allegorical absurdity in order to deny the need for sacrifice, or recognize that the Messiah came two thousand years ago and made the ultimate, permanent sacrifice for sins which the animal offerings merely prefigured. My friend, your wife had better rethink her own religion."

Clyde stared at me hard across the table. By this time both of us had forgotten our self-imposed assignment.

"I'm not a Rabbi," he said, voicing the obvious. "I wouldn't know about that."

"Neither am I," I reminded him, "but I would. Even the prophet Isaiah spoke later of the Messiah who would be 'pierced through for our false steps' and 'crushed for our iniquities.' Most Rabbis interpret that portion of Isaiah 53 as referring to Israel itself, but their rendering comes out a might strange. When Isaiah rejoices that 'by His whipping we are healed,' we'd have to see the society beaten bloody to heal those individuals forming it. And beyond that, when 'He was cut off from the land of the living for the false step of my people to whom the stroke was due,' we'd have to imagine the nation annihilated collectively but the people in it left unharmed. That, Clyde, just doesn't happen. Isaiah preached the need for a personal not a national Messiah. Both you and your wife need one."

"My question," Pollard repeated doggedly, "was how the

loving God Christians preach could send a Jew to hell..."

"... for rejecting Christ as Messiah. Yes, I know. How can a loving judge send a bank robber to jail?"

"That's different!" the agent responded heatedly. "The man's guilty of..."

"Precisely," I cut him off. "The man is guilty, and the judge may be a loving fellow, but he judges based on legal standards. Isn't that an exact parallel with your wife's situation? She values her heritage and her people's traditions. She feels that to accept Christ or to even consider that Jesus might be the Christ would be to betray her people, even though the Old Testament law declares her guilty as it declares us all guilty."

Pollard drummed his fingers on the stack of paperwork.

"I have the distinct feeling," he complained, "that you're twisting my words. Let me slowly, carefully rephrase my question."

"Of course."

He paused to assemble his thoughts. "Why couldn't the Christian God love Jews enough since they believe in Him to declare them righteous whether or not they accept Jesus as Messiah?"

I smiled. "For the same reason that the Jewish God sent His own people into captivity because they professed to believe in Him but chose to disobey Him. God sets the rules. That's His prerogative. We have no right to create our own convenient standards and then criticize Him because our rules differ from His. You think you're undermining evangelical Christianity with your questions, but you're also assailing orthodox Judaism since neither religion teaches universal salvation. You really suggest that God, to satisfy you, must show compassion at the expense of righteousness. I assure you that if He's not righteous, His compassion means nothing. His righteousness demands that sin be punished. His compassion provided Someone to suffer that punishment for us. His righteousness demands personal responsibility for sin. His compassion invites us to personally accept the Savior. That's how He reconciles His love and righteousness. If you were God, how would you do it?"

"I'm not God," Pollard protested. "How would I know? But godly Jews should go to heaven."

"Godly Jews do," I agreed, "because they still have a blood sacrifice for their sins—the Messiah. Everyone else has apostatized from historic orthodoxy whether he realizes it or not. Leviticus actually orders that those who refuse to offer blood sacrifices be cut off from their people! Where does that leave today's Judaism?

"Let's suppose for the sake of argument that God did allow those *you* feel are godly Jews into heaven. What would happen? They'd be confronted while still sinners by a totally holy God. That would be rather like dining at the White House uninvited. Heaven would be hell for the man who didn't already have a little piece of heaven in his soul. Men become holy in God's eyes through accepting the Messiah's sacrifice, and unholy men might well be more miserable in heaven than in hell."

I stared at him until he glanced away. "Constant scrutiny can make one extremely uneasy, can't it? The Bible talks about fire, pain and wailing in hell where sinners experience God's righteous justice. We don't know, however, how those same sinners would react or what they would feel in heaven where man is meant to enjoy a breathtakingly close relationship with God. They might wither under the scrutiny and even beg for hell."

"Nuts!" Pollard reacted. "If you're going to downgrade heaven to squirm out of answering, then let's forget it. I think you've been taking wiseacre lessons from that partner of yours."

I glanced down to identify the next dossier. "He has influenced my thinking a bit," I acknowledged. "I believe he used substantially that same argument five years ago in Barcelona when we recovered a million pounds worth of diamonds for an Israeli businessman. The gentleman, incidentally, committed his life to the Messiah, so I don't think

160

he considered the comments on heaven, as you so quaintly put it, 'wiseacre.' "

Agent Pollard managed a growl deep in his throat but had now evidently decided to keep his mouth closed and his lips sealed. He concentrated on the page in front of him and retreated into the same shell that we'd encountered on the trip to the National Gallery. It was interesting, to say the least, that he didn't get up and leave altogether.

I used the opportunity to pray for Geoff's safe return, then went back to my job scrutinizing the lives of men who, even in normal times, lived under a microscope. For the most part the indiscretions were rather ordinary. A couple had overdue traffic tickets. Here and there I ran across an anti-war activist who had mellowed and become part of the establishment. Required congressional financial disclosures weren't always complete. Rumors of conflict of interest occasionally marred an official's image. A handful of marriages seemed shaky. Perhaps the most often repeated indiscretion was drunkenness. Several senators and representatives had evidently fallen victim to the diplomatic cocktail party circuit.

"This fellow Lonnie Carlyle," I mentioned in an effort to break the ice, "should have an interesting time of it if he ever runs for something. Three engagements broken . . . two DWI arrests . . . he's even been named correspondent in a divorce case. The Carlyle family would have to spend a fortune to put the best face on that."

Pollard got up to pour himself a cup of something hot. "They've got it to spend," he pronounced. "There was a big profit margin for bathtub gin during prohibition. The grandfather tries to live that down now, but Lonnie's more interested in living it up. I met him on a case once. He's a real airhead."

"That's tea in the pot," I volunteered. "If you prefer coffee, pour the tea into a pitcher and use the pot for boiling water. Sorry we've only got instant."

"No matter. Instant's fine." He sprinkled first coffee crystals then creamer from jar to stoneware cup without measuring. "Powdered coffee...powdered milk...in a styrofoam container. That's the way I like it. You know what really makes good coffee?"

I was intrigued with the recipe. "No. What?"

"Pour your hot water directly out of the tap. That way all your salts and sludge have settled to the bottom of the heater tank." He demonstrated by pouring a cupful. "Of course, during the energy crisis people turned their heaters down and the coffee wasn't hot enough, but it's better now."

I half expected the gentleman to stir with his finger, but he did his duty with a spoon and then settled down across from me again to sip and read.

"This guy Jacob Manville," he noted irritably, "seems too good to be true. He doesn't smoke, doesn't drink, doesn't chew. He married his high school sweetheart and worked his way through college designing computer software. When he served as ambassador to Yugoslavia, he actually tried to learn Yugoslavian."

"Serbo-Croatian."

"What?"

"Yugoslavians speak Serbo-Croatian, along with a couple of other languages."

"You don't say," He crossed out an entry and penned in the correction. "Anyway, this guy sounds like a phony. I'd watch out for him. Nobody's that good unless he's up to something."

"An interesting hypothesis," I mused. "I'll file that for future reference right next to your coffee recipe."

"You're welcome to it," Pollard acknowledged. "That Lillian Billings is another one you've got to watch for. Did you know she actually paid to have her husband's operation done at her company's hospital when he could have had it free at Bethesda Naval at the taxpayer's expense? She also gives excessively to charities. I mean we're talking way over ten percent. I wonder what her angle is."

"Perhaps," I suggested, "she's a humanitarian."

"Naw," Pollard disagreed. "You can deep six that idea.

162

Her company doesn't sell consumer items. What kind of ad could she run? 'Buy your rocket engines and artificial legs from us. We support the Boy Scouts.' It wouldn't be good business."

I shuddered inwardly at the man's reasoning.

"Red . . . " I decided to use his nickname, "you sound like a big city newspaper reporter at his jaded worst. Always looking for angles . . . cynical . . . . Have you ever thought that the lady just might take pleasure in helping people without thought of . . . "

We both froze at the sound of a key turning in the door lock. Pollard eased the gun out of his shoulder holster.

Geoff's cheerful voice, however, floated in from the hallway. "No need to stop talking on my account. I already heard what Christmas present you're getting me."

He came striding jauntily into the apartment with a couple of books under his arm as Red reholstered his pistol.

"What an utterly delightful evening," Geoff declared with fresh-as-a-daisy exuberance. "Those Tucker ladies did such a marvelous job on the dolls and costumes. I've never seen 'The Tempest' performed better either. The play was in every respect excellent!"

Pollard yawned and appraised my partner with obvious resentment at his wakefulness.

"The intermissions mustn't have been bad either," he groused, "unless you've taken to wearing lipstick. If you have, you should spread it more evenly next time."

Geoff, somewhat ruefully, pulled a handkerchief from his pocket and wiped his lips. He refused, however, to be intimidated out of his mood.

"Ah, Clyde," he bantered, "you have such verbal polish, such uncanny charm. I'm sure the snake dances to your tune unwaveringly. Better have those eyes checked, though. In case you haven't noticed, I wear a goatee and . . . "

"I wasn't aware," I interrupted hastily, "that Shakespeare put any dolls in 'The Tempest.' "

"He didn't," Geoff conceded. "They made a slight

163

adaptation. Paloma really loved them. A few reminded her of work done by Mexican artisans. After the show we stood out front for hours talking about our respective cultures' accomplishments in the field of . . . "

"Lucky for you," Pollard broke in, "you weren't blown away standing there. I've heard of fool moves in my time, but setting yourself up as a target and then going public without a tail takes the cake."

"The news is out," I informed Geoff, "about that joint meeting. We would have given you protection when we found out, but we had no idea where to look."

My partner didn't show the slightest concern. "I rather suspected," he mused, "that that might have happened."

"You suspected!" I was appalled. "You deliberately risked . . . "

"Hold it!" Geoff held up his free hand for quiet. "I suspected because of all the vagrant plain clothesmen that have taken to lounging on this block. Paloma and I were right across the street all the time at the Shakespeare Library. It seems they feature the Bard there in drama as well as print. You've done a commendable job, Clyde, in stationing your men. Miss Guerrero and I watched them take their stations with the greatest interest while we chatted. We were, of course, in no real danger since all the attention was focused away from us by your army of the nondescript."

"I should have guessed," I acknowledged with relief. "You didn't have any library books with you when you left."

"Except," my partner corrected, "that they're not from across the street. Paloma picked them up for me at a quaint little used book shoppe out in Riverdale." He held aloft a small leatherbound volume as though it were a prize. "*Paley's Natural Theology*, 1850 edition. It only cost her thirty-five cents. The criminology book was a real find, too. We'll have to stop by there for a browse before we return to England."

He changed expressions as though reminded of an unpleasantness.

164

"You know, John, I'm beginning to dread that farewell. I've never known anyone quite like her before, and frankly I feel very . . . drawn to her. Perhaps that's because of those prayers she was embarrassed about mentioning. She's so alive, so tender, and intelligent. Did you know she actually enjoys hang gliding?"

"And you would," I responded skeptically, "consider that a mark of intelligence?"

He looked at me reproachfully. "Not of intelligence. But certainly of pluck, and a daring sense of adventure. She's a dabbler like myself with an insatiable curiosity that . . . "

"By George," Pollard broke in with a mock British accent, "I think he's got it. I think he's caught it. I think he's, how should I say it, 'grown accustomed to her face.' " He dropped the accent as a bad job. "You English are so insanely reserved. Why don't you just admit to yourself you love her, and then we can cut the gaff and get back down to cases. For a detective you're sure not very perceptive when it comes to your own . . . . "

A shot rang out on the street followed by loud semi-automatic bursts and policemen yelling instructions back and forth to each other. Geoff started for the door, but Pollard sprang on him and wrestled him to the floor. I decided to duck also as the front window shattered and machine gun fire sprayed holes in plaster around the room.

"Stay down," Pollard shouted, "Guns out, but no movement. These vermin are after you. Don't draw their fire."

The building shook from a deafening explosion and flames shot heavenward just outside the window. The concussion knocked me flat on my face.

"Move!" Pollard screamed. "Wiggle to the bathroom where there's some protection. Let's hope they're out of grenades."

As if in answer, a blast across the street set my ears to ringing. We started crawling in the direction he'd indicated.

165

This wasn't a police action. It was war.

"Shouldn't we stay here and add to the fire power? Any commando could get inside the building and...."

Heavy fire from the street drowned out my words.

"Let's do what he says, John, and fast," Weston chimed in. "The man has combat experience and he's planned for contingencies."

Right then a bullet ricocheted off the teapot and tatooed the wall just over my head. I scurried for all I was worth. It's amazing how fast one can move on his stomach when he must. In a few seconds we were huddled on the bathroom floor listening to the sound of carnage outside. Explosion followed explosion. Police sirens wailed in the distance. We choked on plaster dust as someone lobbed a grenade into one of the apartments above us and knocked half our ceiling loose. The rat-tat-tat of automatic rifles, machine pistols, and who knows what else cut through the air in frenzied bursts that never quite subsided to stillness. The pungent smell of cordite crept under the door and assailed our nostrils.

Pollard unclipped a walkie talkie from his belt as he slouched in the corner with his back against the bathtub.

"Shepherd to Watchdog," he breathed into the mouthpiece. "Hennessy, what's happening out there?"

Hiss and static provided the initial response, then "Watchdog's" voice became barely intelligible above distorted battle sounds.

"Sir, they have got us outmanned and outgunned but we've got position on them. I don't know how many there are, but Russell's picked off three from his spot on the library roof before they could... can't finish, I'll get back with you..."

Another voice broke urgently through the hiss. "Eagle's Nest One to Three. Charlie, there's a black van approaching fast. Pick it off before it gets too close. It's probably packed with commandos or enough dynamite to blow the whole blasted block. Nest Two... Nest Two... Do you read me? Nest Two..."

We could make out sniper fire followed by a tire squeal

and the metallic scream of a crumpling front end. There was no explosion.

"Nest Three to One. Nobody's coming out. I think we got 'em. Nest One, do you read? Ground six . . . "

Pollard turned down the volume on his walkie talkie and looked at us bleakly.

"Smitty's Nest One on the roof over us. A real swell guy . . . . Nest Two's in the library. Looks like both of them are gone. I hope the city's SWAT team shows up pretty quick because we sure can't put down much of a crossfire out front."

"Those sirens tell the story," I assured him. "Help's on the way."

We all went flat as a loud thud emanated from the living room. No further sounds followed, however, aside from the constant sporadic small arms fire in the streets.

"Lord," my partner prayed quietly, "let Your will be done. If we don't make it through, please replace us with somebody who can solve this case. Take care of Paloma."

"Nice sentiments," Pollard acknowledged as he propped himself back up in the corner. "Let's see if I can raise Hennessy." He turned the volume up and pressed the talk button. "Shepherd to Watchdog. Shepherd to Watchdog . . . "

There wasn't any answer. Even Nest Three was silent now.

"The emergency plan," Clyde noted almost to himself, "was for our men to form a small protective pocket around this building. They may have dropped radios while dodging bullets or dragging out the wounded. The attackers are probably holed up in some row houses next door or across the street. When the SWAT team's in place, the commandos should be sandwiched. Should be . . . " He stopped in mid sentence.

We dug in mentally and waited without the faintest glimmer of what was happening outside. The moments oozed by in slow motion for the better part of an hour. Once the shooting actually seemed to tail off almost to the point of extinction. Then the air outside erupted into renewed fury which reached a crescendo before subsiding. As quickly as it had begun, the shooting stopped. We sat and waited.

"Those poor lads on the force," Geoff breathed. "It's such a strange feeling to know men are dying all around you and there isn't a thing you can do about it. How stupid of me to have started outside to help. We would have been useless."

"Worse than useless," Pollard concurred. "Assuming our side has won, we'd better stay put until they do a house to house for snipers."

"Well," I noted shakily, "you jolly well got your reaction from the killer, Geoff. But who thought it would be this?"

"Who indeed?" Weston observed bleakly. "Who indeed?"

We heard a banging at the front door to the apartment but our ears had become so used to explosions that its significance didn't register. Then the pounding was followed up by a voice.

"Sir, this is Hennessy. Are you all right in there?"

We regained our feet and Pollard opened the door to our inner sanctum.

"Yeah," he yelled. "Is it safe to come out?"

"You'd better hurry, sir," Hennessy shouted. "There's a fire in the next building and it's headed this way."

At this point Weston asserted command. "Let's grab what we can fast, then," he directed. "John, you gather whatever personal effects we may have left. Clyde, you help me with the evidence. We'll need all those papers you brought, all your notes, and as many shoes as we can rescue. If we have to, we'll make several trips and stack things up on the sidewalk. Get cracking men, there isn't a moment to lose."

Red was a quick thinker under pressure. He hurried from the bathroom to the shattered front window under which I'd stacked the smelly shoes and began tossing them un-ceremoniously out into the street. Geoff gathered up the scattered papers and his two books, which were dusty but otherwise undamaged. I stuffed suitcases, grabbed up our briefcase laboratory, which sported three bullet holes in its side, stepped over a backpack I'd never seen before, and rescued the rat cage. When Clyde had finished disposing of the shoes, we drew our weapons, and ventured outside to the street.

The sight that met our eyes was incredible. In the flickering red glow from the building next door, and the harsh beams of spotlights stationed at both ends of the block, we could make out the hulks of three or four automobiles, some still burning, which had been parked in front of or near our building. I couldn't even tell which one had been our Cadillac. Forty-year-old maples were badly scarred. Across the street large chunks of marble had been knocked off the Folger Shakespeare Library and, of the two thespian faces on its front, only the sad one remained. The buildings to both sides of ours had sustained severe damage to the bottom floors. The three of us stood and looked about in open-mouthed fascination at the devastation as police in fatigues with rifles at ready kept a wary eye out for suspicious movement anywhere. A few feet away a commando lay chest up with an expression more of surprise than of pain sculpted by death on her face. Her bloodless olive skin blended with the camouflage uniform except for the numerous spots now stained red. I wondered which high school she'd attended. Was this mere youngster the mysterious swarthy woman who'd dropped a cigarette behind the shoe shop? An acrid cloud of smoke momentarily enveloped us, and I fought back nausea as I turned away from her. I silently thanked God that Pollard had sequestered us rather than directing us out here to shoot children. Her companions were probably older, I mused, but that didn't really make much difference. How many of both sides' dead were still screaming in another dimension?

Hennessy, who'd evidently been upstairs warning anyone else he could find in our building, came running out behind us. I noticed he had what looked like a Russian-made machine pistol in his hand.

"Sir," he shouted at Pollard, "it's not safe for you all to stay here. Paramedics and firemen are on their way, and we won't be able to keep the area secured when they start driving through the line. My orders are to get you out of here."

"Sounds sensible," Clyde responded. "What do we use for transportation?"

"It's over there." Hennessy pointed to a hearse double parked by a smoldering wreck across the street. "Anyone laying for you outside our perimeter shouldn't bother with that. I'll be riding shotgun."

"Good idea," Weston agreed. "What about those shoes over there? We'll need them as evidence."

Pollard's assistant followed the line of Geoff's extended finger to the scattered pile of mutilated footwear.

"They'll be taken care of," he assured us. "The important thing now is to get you away from the area and stashed in a safe house. Let's go."

The fellow broke into a trot toward the hearse, and we were obliged to imitate him as best we could while struggling with our bags and papers. By the time we got there he had the rear door open. Each of us haphazardly slung his materials inside and hopped in after them. Hennessy slammed the door behind us, then entered the front seat on the passenger side. The driver started forward and we began weaving our way around wrecked motorcars, tree branches and dead bodies.

"Be sure to lie flat," Hennessy reminded us without looking back.

"Right now I feel flat," Geoff responded. "How many FBI'ers died?"

The agent spoke stoically. "We lost four or five. We've got several wounded. The local police with us at the beginning were shot up, too. None of us were prepared for the heavy stuff they rolled out. It's a miracle you guys made it. I saw a block buster flung into your window, but it must have been a dud."

"A block buster?" I queried. "That wouldn't look anything like a knapsack, would it?"

Goose bumps ran up and down my spine as I saw the back of Hennessy's head bob in the shadows.

"You got it."

"How fortunate," I responded somewhat shakily, "that I didn't pack it to the hearse with us. That would have been rather a sticky wicket."

"What about the attackers?" Geoff prompted Pollard's assistant. "Were you able to take prisoners?"

Lights flickered across the fabric ceiling as we slowed at the perimeter. Hennessy passed on instructions about the footwear and we were waved through.

"It was a suicide squad," he resumed. "We've got three or four wounded, but there's a fifty-fifty chance they'll wind up DOA."

"Just great!" Weston pounded the floor in his frustration. "John, when we get wherever we're going, the two of us will have to devour those dossiers. What about your tests on the shoes?"

"Essentially negative," I admitted. "They all had substantially the same wear and battery charge levels. All, of course, except Johnson's. Throckingham, it turns out, didn't have any of the shoes, so maybe the plot *was* to wipe out the innovators in Congress.

Geoff slowly relaxed. "Perhaps, old bean, it was. I wonder..." He remained silent for so long I began to wonder if he'd succumbed to the day's hectic pace and fallen asleep. "We'd better," he finally spoke, "get in touch with that colonel again about some equipment we'll need. Let me think this through. Yes, there's going to have to be some international coordination. I think I may have finally figured this whole mess out. There are still a couple of pieces missing in the puzzle, but I'm hoping we'll find them in that mountain of paper. What a shame so many had to die when the answer was right there staring us in the face all along."

The engine purred powerfully under the bonnet as our hearse sped through the night toward a safe haven and, beyond that, an appointment with destiny. It was a long ride and eventually Geoff, Clyde and I fell into a fitful sleep.

14
THE CALCULATED RISK

The government set us up that weekend in a farmhouse near Fallston, north of Baltimore. Soldiers from nearby Aberdeen Proving Ground patrolled the fifty yards between us and the woods. The place, in fact, reminded me more of a command post than a safe house since we certainly weren't idling away our time before the congressional appearance. Geoff was constantly calling someone or other on a bank of phones which relayed through switchboards elsewhere so they couldn't be traced.

Because of the violence of the attack on us, security was beefed up around major government buildings. Col. Claypool was put on special assignment by the Pentagon to head up military activities related to the case and my partner was in almost constant communication with him. Some of their talks were so hush hush that the scramble phone was used, everyone was escorted from the room, and jamming sounds were broadcast over outside speakers in case someone had a parabolic microphone aimed our way. Weston, in his official capacity with the FBI, also used every agent available to further a civilian investigation. New information was, however, still a rare commodity. We were after some sort of ruthless, faceless monster who struck from anonymity and took every conceivable step to stay in the shadows.

Reports coming in, though, proved Weston had been right in suspecting the manner of Amy Sheldon's death. The catheter removed from her artery seemed in every sense normal, but when we heated it in water to 98.6°, it squeezed closed in the center like a motorcar thermostat. On closer inspection we found that it contained an almost microscopic circuit which, on a certain radio signal, had initially triggered the mechanism. Then, as the victim's body cooled, the tube reopened automatically. Unfortunately we were unable to find anyone even remotely connected with the investigation who had bought transmitting equipment of that frequency. The catheter itself proved untraceable and the surgeon who implanted it had evidently had no idea of what he was doing.

Geoff may have said he'd "figured the mess out" but that didn't stop him from ordering a wild array of background checks on everyone from Throckingham, Carlyle, the Billings, Jarvis, Manville and Johnson, to Col. Claypool, Paloma's father, and even Cathleen Strong. Our murderer was under some rock, and Weston seemed determined to leave no stone unturned in identifying him—or her. Twelve of the twenty commandos killed outside our apartment had been identified as government employees, and that revelation had sent Washington into a state of near paranoia. Moles were suspected everywhere.

Our only respite was a trip to church on Sunday morning in spite of military objections. I wondered who the friendly folk at Grace Bible Church thought we were when fifty of us, some in uniform and some with bulging suit coats, took up every empty seat in the building. They would have been even more curious if they'd seen the back-up vehicles parked out of sight and the troops patrolling the woods. We, however, who knew all about the precautions, didn't give them a second thought and thoroughly enjoyed the worship service. I noticed that Clyde Pollard was listening intently.

Monday morning we were whisked into the Capitol building through an underground garage before dawn. The military wasn't taking any chances. We had to cool our heels in a mahogany paneled anteroom off the House chamber for several hours. It was a beautiful opportunity to rehearse, perspire, and pray. Our coterie did a good bit of all three.

"It's almost time," Clyde finally interrupted our silent deliberations. "I hope you know what you're doing."

Geoff nodded seriously. "We'll most assuredly find out in a minute," he observed, "won't we? You've got the House cameras switched over from live broadcast to videotape?"

Pollard didn't even glance down at his checklist. "Don't worry. Everything's been taken care of. You guys have your little show complete with invited guests, witnesses, and everything but a script."

"What about the library? Have you got agents stationed?"

"I said don't worry. That aspect sounds like a fool's errand to me, but we've carried out your orders."

Geoff straightened his jacket and picked up his briefcase. "Well, then, gentlemen, I suggest we proceed."

We walked down an elaborate but totally empty corridor to a mahogany door which sported diamond-shaped glass panels separated by gold-leaf supports. A wizened gentleman in formal attire preceded us through.

"Mr. Speaker," he called, "I present to you Mr. Geoffrey Weston and John Taylor, consulting detectives."

It hardly called for it, the way we'd botched matters, but the entire body arose as one and greeted us with hearty applause. As Pollard and two other agents took up stations in the rear, Geoff and I walked down plush blue carpeting toward the front, shaking extended hands as we went. It was a heady experience even if the galleries on all sides above us were uncharacteristically empty. The imposing three-tiered platform loomed before us.

As if in a dream we followed our briefing instructions and mounted to the long mahogany desk on the second tier. The large-boned Vice President of the United States stood directly behind me on the top tier next to the Speaker of the House. Speaker Jarvis banged his gavel and Geoff and I took our seats, as did everyone else in the hall.

"Ladies and gentlemen, Mr. Geoffrey Weston."

My partner got somewhat self-consciously to his feet and approached the podium. Meanwhile I looked out at the sea of people seated before me on row after row of semi-circular benches padded in rich maroon leather. Senators sat in the front sections, or at least printed signs pasted to bench backs indicated that rank. I recognized a couple. Jacob Manville with his gray hair and strong chin was unmistakable in the second row. Desmond Billings looked up at us from under his thick brows. His wheelchair had been parked front row center. Billy Bob Throckingham had stored away his cigars, but his paunch and Churchillian double chin gave him away instantly. Carl Johnson was visible further back among his house colleagues.

Up front to the right, chairs had been set up for certain individuals whose presence Geoff had requested. Augustin Guerrero, Mexico's President, was seated next to his daughter and an interpreter. Harrison Dodd, Lillian Billings, and Col. Claypool sat immediately behind them.

"Mr. Speaker, Mr. President, distinguished guests, ladies and gentlemen," Weston intoned the ritual, "it's an honor to be here before you today, and I assure you that I have not requested that honor lightly. Nor has it been received lightly in certain circles."

A strained laugh greeted his reference to Friday night. As he paused for it to subside he stroked his goatee thoughtfully.

"One of you out there," he continued, "is a murderer. You know who you are. You know I know who you are. I'll give you just one chance to declare yourself and save us all trouble."

The silence which met his request was so thick it could have been cut with a butter knife and served up with tea.

"Very well," Geoff concluded, "we'll go about it the hard way. There are, after all, only a handful of people here who could even be construed to have a motive for Jim Strong's death. Let's stick to that one crime, at least initially, to simplify matters."

As my partner glanced around the room, he now seemed decidedly more at ease and warming to his subject.

"The first suspect chronologically," he observed, "was the distinguished President of Mexico, Augustin Guerrero."

When Augustin heard the translation, even the pinstripes

on his suit stiffened, but he maintained stoic silence as he gazed our way.

"The line of reasoning," Geoff continued, "was to the effect that Strong stood in the way of a critical arms deal and had to be removed. Augustin had motive. He had opportunity since his embassy staff could have arranged attempts on my life both here and in London. He may or may not have had the scientific expertise available. A close friend, Ricardo Delgado Soto, ran the Comodo Shoe Company which . . . "

Augustin, no longer able to restrain himself, jumped to his feet. "*Es mentira, pura mentira!* How could you, my friend, say such a lie. I did not even know the man."

Geoff looked down from the podium, clearly surprised at our former client's outburst. "*Claro,*" he spoke briefly in Spanish, "of course you didn't. Please sit down and hear me out. I haven't accused you of anything."

Augustin started to say something further, then thought better of it and resumed an uneasy vigil from his chair.

"As I was saying, ladies and gentlemen," Geoff declared, "the President was a friend of Ricardo Delgado Soto who ran the Comodo Shoe Company which supplied the ready-made models of the footwear which you subsequently bought. But at this point the motive self-destructs. Fully two-thirds of all congressmen received advertising brochures or actually bought the shoes. An equal number were on both sides of the arms sale issue. Neither Augustin nor the Mexican government could, therefore, have been implicated in the murders. Even in the unlikely event they'd secretly planned to use the weapons against the U.S. rather than against the rebels, they certainly wouldn't have done anything to endanger that aid package.

"It's interesting to note, furthermore, that when I was able to make out the Mexican connection in this puzzle, it showed itself to be decidedly anti-government. I arranged a meeting with Augustin's daughter, Paloma, in such a way as to insure the killer's scrutiny. He assumed, as I knew he would, that incriminating information was being passed along a chain from the elder Soto to his son to Paloma—who was present when warning shots were fired at the son—and ultimately to me. If the Soto family couldn't be frightened into silence, they'd have to be liquidated before they could open up the company books and provide proof of any allegations.

"Co-conspirators in Mexico, therefore, very obligingly tried to assassinate the family and destroy any evidence. I'd counted on that. The Sotos' would-be assassins, ladies and gentlemen, turned out to be communist guerillas. It was not Augustin, therefore, but his sworn enemies who were involved somehow in Strong's death. So much for one suspect. Please forgive me, sir, for running you through an emotional ringer. Now who else had a motive?"

He gazed down front directly at Billy Bob Throckingham and pointed with a casual gesture.

"You, Senator Throckingham, are a political opportunist and make no bones about it. You were, furthermore, viewed by Jim Strong and his wife as a definite moral liability. The king maker was a necessary evil during the campaign, but would he be able to retain power after Strong's election? Doubtful. You could well have decided to replace the candidate with someone a bit more flexible. You also employed Amy Sheldon in your office. That lady, of course, showed up on our doorstep to poison us shortly after we'd given you our address."

Billy Bob didn't so much as uncross his legs. "I did not, suh," he projected with practiced ease, "hira her ta do that! She was an aide and nothin' mo'."

"Well stated, Senator," Geoff acknowledged as he raised congressional eyebrows by tearing open a packet of peanuts and pouring half its contents into his mouth. "You are," he managed around the nuts, "of course, correct. If she'd had our address, she would have appeared on the scene sooner and wouldn't have been checking every recently vacant apartment. You are also, for all your wheeling and dealing, a legitimate conservative and I somehow can't visualize you trying to give a hotfoot to most of your right wing colleagues.

177

That would have rather spoiled the wheeler dealer game for you, I should think. Why then were you left out when it came to being offered those deadly shoes? Was the ad lost in the mail, or did the killer, perhaps, have a soft spot for certain kinds of politicians? That last is, I believe, the answer. You weren't perceived as posing a threat to the murderer's plans, whatever they were. You certainly aren't the murderer."

Billy Bob seemed relieved but also vaguely annoyed as he mopped his brow with a wrinkled handkerchief.

"Thank you, suh," he declared, "for the vote of confidence, but ah reserve the right ta disagree on the matta' of whether Ah'm a threat to the murdera'."

Weston answered with only a nod. His eyes focused on one then another legislator in the audience with penetrating appraisal.

"What, though, were those plans?" he asked rhetorically. "What would motivate an indiscriminate attack against two-thirds of Congress? What would precipitate a cowardly crime such as blowing an airliner filled with innocent people out of the sky? What nefarious scheme would prompt someone to marshal twenty-four commandos to wipe out one apartment building?" My partner pointed his index finger skyward. "Only one explanation, gentlemen, makes any sense at all. High treason! Our killer was concerned only secondarily with Mexico. His primary objective was to overthrow the United States government. To that end he sought to keep Congress in a turmoil through random lightning strikes while he brought together other elements in his plot. Those elements included the services of this country's sworn enemies and the judicious use of a dazzling array of deadly gadgetry.

"Now that gadgetry is, in itself, a puzzle. We've been able to trace *none* of it. It wasn't manufactured behind the Iron Curtain since every component appears to be American or Oriental. Yet it was *manufactured*, not simply pasted together in some garage workshop. Who would have had the wherewithal to do that? The mob, perhaps? One or two criminal cartels do own foreign plants for bootlegging name-brand electronics. The underworld is, however, extremely patriotic. Even members of international crime brotherhoods tend to pride themselves on being Americans. What's more, organized crime has no reason to overthrow the government. Business is as good as ever. Why rock the boat?

"No, gentlemen, it wasn't the mob. One of you must have legitimate business connections which enabled you to get what you wanted rather handily. Nearly all of you, of course, receive hefty business support. Some have come to these halls from the presidency of large corporations. Though not a member of this club, Mr. Dodd, I believe, currently heads up a large chemical firm and keeps his finger actively in politics."

Dodd came to his feet almost instantly. "Mr. Speaker," he addressed Jarvis impassionedly, "how much longer are we to be subjected to this witchhunt? Weston well knows my company doesn't deal in electronics. I don't see why he should be allowed to bandy around accusations for dramatic effect."

Jarvis banged his gavel and leaned forward over his desk on the top tier.

"Mr. Dodd," he admonished, "you are out of order. Mr. Weston has the floor. We're going to get to the bottom of this messy business and not be sidetracked by a lot of interruptions. Please sit down."

Dodd glared at the Speaker but remained stationary as a statue.

"Either sit," Jarvis thundered, "or you'll be cited for contempt of Congress."

A mole on the industrialist's left cheek twitched involuntarily. The fellow clearly wasn't used to taking orders. He cleared his throat.

"But Mr. Speaker . . . "

Seeing Representative Jarvis's gavel rise ever so slightly, he hurriedly retreated to the safety of his chair.

Geoff glanced appreciatively over his shoulder at his defender then resumed eye contact with Harrison Dodd.

"Thank you, Mr. Speaker," he continued. "And Mr. Dodd,

rest assured that I'm bringing up these matters not merely to unmask the guilty but also to exonerate the innocent. You'll remember how, following the Kennedy assassination, there were years of speculation about possible accomplices. I don't want that to happen here. Speculations laid to rest now should stay at rest. At least that's the hope."

Geoff shifted his attention to include the entire assembly.

"Harrison Dodd, ladies and gentlemen, has reacted as intensely as he has because he knows that Strong and Kidd voted to preserve some endangered minnows and thereby forced one of his plants to install expensive anti-pollution equipment. He's also aware that he's not nearly so far removed from the electronics industry as he claims since he supplies a partially owned subsidary with chemical raw materials for making certain electrical components. However, this case has gone far beyond being a simple double murder, and the man's hypothetical motive can't be extended by any means, no matter how farfetched, to include the entire murderous rampage we've witnessed. I'm afraid, sir, that we'll have to cross you from our list."

Dodd's cheek stopped twitching, but aside from that, his expression didn't soften. He did, however, slouch a bit in the chair.

Geoff paused for a sip of water.

"Lillian Billings," he noted soberly, "is another kettle of fish entirely. She has direct control of International Bionics and Aerospace which most certainly could have produced the lightning attractors, electronic catheters and bugs which have been plaguing us. The firm's international nature would also give her connections in places like Mexico City and London. You do have branches there, don't you Mrs. Billings?"

"We do," she spoke out loudly from the temporary section, "have a plant in Mexico City. There's only an affiliated sales office in London."

Geoff smiled politely at the frowsy blond whose nondescript appearance belied her tremendous ability.

"Close enough, madam. You know, if one pushes hard enough, it's even possible to imagine a motive for you. While on one of your junkets as a trade representative to the USSR, you could have been approached...."

"That's a pernicious lie!" her husband broke in heatedly. He fairly stared daggers at Weston from his wheelchair directly in front of the podium. "Lillian would never do a thing to hurt this country. She loves it. She'd die for it. How dare you invade these shores and besmirch the reputations of solid Americans who have built this land with their sweat, tears, and...."

"I'd never do that!" Geoff overrode him with his own firm voice. "Your wife has, however, done horrible damage to this country."

"You despicable, scummy toad! How has she...."

"By trusting you!" my partner cut him off. "You're the traitor! You're the murderer! She followed your recommendations and hired your agents for her company."

Desmond Billings recoiled as though he'd been struck.

"You..." he gritted his teeth. "You are in for the largest libel suit you've ever heard of. I'll have you know I've served my country faithfully in this very building for nearly two decades!"

"And," Geoff added, "betrayed it every evening when you went home. Billings, your little show of righteous outrage won't do you a bit of good. I think you really were successful in hiding your treason from your wife, but you haven't from me."

The Senator pounded his fist on the portable desk top fitted to his wheelchair. "Prove it! Prove it, I dare you!"

"Why certainly." Geoff frowned and stroked his goatee like some college professor about to answer a student's impertinent challenge. "Where shall I start in the litany of your errors? Ah, yes. Perhaps the clumsiest was your attempt to bug our apartment by sticking a listening device to that lamp. We had a fairly competent bunch of chaps guarding the building, you know. At first I thought they might have

181

slipped up, but then I realized it was more likely that someone attending my little demonstration had brought it in with him. Now who could that be? We'd checked credentials carefully. The reporters were all on the up and up, and they were too far removed from the case to have a motive. That left the politicians. If the bug had been planted high up behind a picture, I would have said to myself, 'now that rules out Senator Billings because he couldn't reach that far above his chair and he'd be too conspicuous trying to do the job on crutches.' However, Senator, the bug was planted at a height very convenient for someone seated as you are now."

Billings's eyes narrowed as he studied his opponent. "That," he fairly spat out, "proves nothing. The room was crowded. If there was something planted, anyone could have done it. I certainly didn't."

"Oh," Geoff disagreed, "but you did. It's true, of course, that I can't prove it, but your move was still the height of folly because it drastically shortened my list of suspects. Up until that point anyone in the city could have been responsible. Once the field was reduced, everything began pointing in your direction."

Furrows deepened above Desmond's bushy eyebrows. "Like what?"

"Oh," Geoff obliged, "like the fact that James Strong had recently taken out a book on the symptoms and cures of psychotic diseases. You're the only congressman, you'll admit, who has undergone a brain operation. He also borrowed a volume entitled *Spinoffs of Space Technology*. Doesn't that sound just a might like he had your wife's company in mind?"

"Maybe," Billings conceded, "but not necessarily. And these men around you will attest to the fact I'm no psychotic." His voice brimmed over with sarcasm. "You're burying yourself, Mr. Weston. Please proceed. Everything you say will make dandy weapons in court."

A smile flickered at the edges of Geoff's mouth. "My, Desmond, but you are calculating."

Rather unaccountably Billings drew back slightly in his chair as though he'd felt my partner's casual jibe almost physically.

"Yes," Geoff answered the reaction, "I do know. Senator Strong must have suspected, too. No doubt you would have killed him by some other means if he'd forced a showdown. As it was, the time bomb you'd put on his feet went off before that was necessary, didn't it?

"When you first mentioned your operation I knew, of course, that you were lying. The scar behind your left ear was simply in the wrong place to have resulted from removing a tumor from the brain's motor region. There was a tumor, all right, but it was rooted in the verbal and visual memory centers. The legs are, of course, controlled by a spot nearly on the top of the head next to the central fissure. Why had you lied? At first I thought you'd simply feared political defeat if voters thought your memory had been impaired. You might have even faked the walking problem to give a less damaging reason for the operation. That would account for having the operation at your wife's company hospital. It was necessary to guard against news leaks. You seemed perfectly lucid when I talked to you, though, so I assumed any impairment was slight. At a later time, however, I came to realize that the walking problem wasn't faked. The damage to your brain was simply far more extensive than I'd initially supposed."

Billings half turned in his seat to appeal to his colleagues. "You all know me," he bellowed. "You know I'm not, as he accuses, 'impaired.' This man is the one who's insane. Let's put an end to this travesty!"

"Ah," Geoff shot back, "then you don't want me to 'bury' myself anymore? You don't want fodder for your legal cannons? Could it be because you're afraid?"

"Never!" Billings pounded the desk top again. "I'm insulted, outraged, and . . . what do you think you're doing?"

He paused uncertainly as Geoff disappeared behind the podium to bend down and open his briefcase.

"You are also," Weston responded, "guilty." He emerged with a pair of slightly mutilated shoes firmly in his grasp. He held them aloft. "This, ladies and gentlemen, is the evidence which conclusively proves Desmond's part in the murders."

The crowd responded with a murmur, and the Speaker once again banged his gavel for silence.

Geoff favored the suspect with a withering gaze.

"You know, you really wouldn't do a bad job at murder if you weren't forced to depend on lackeys for your leg work. They lack your own meticulous flare for detail." He set one shoe down on the podium and held the other before him as though he were one of the three wise men bearing treasure.

"When you were sure I'd discovered the secret of the shoes, you realized you could divert attention from yourself by becoming a victim. All you had to do was turn in your own pair of the murderous things. The problem was, of course, that you didn't have any. Your agent had told you how I'd guessed Strong's funeral footwear was fake. You knew you absolutely had to come up with 'something old' rather than 'something new' if you'd have any chance at all of fooling me. So you directed one of those unimaginative lackeys to either latch onto used shoes or pre-wear new ones before sending them to me. As you can see, the fellow followed your directions. He forgot, however, one important detail. These shoes are totally indistinguishable from those handed in to me by other members of Congress. They shouldn't be, though. How does a man confined to a wheelchair put that much wear and tear on a pair of shoes? That's the one uncontrovertible piece of evidence which proves you're a murderer and a traitor."

The Senator had the desperation of a trapped animal now as he looked about for support from among his colleagues. He was met, however, only by silent accusation.

"But . . . but this is preposterous! I . . . . "

His left hand came up from under the wheelchair's writing platform holding a forty-five automatic directed at Weston's heart. All pretense was gone now.

"You may think you have me," he stated icily, "but, the

184

joke's on you. The movement's going to win. I'm going to win! Capitalism is yesterday's garbage, and you along with it. In spite of all your bumbling, you've stumbled onto who I am, but you're a dead man. Your knowledge won't do you or anybody else any good. I'll live on and you'll be buzzard meat."

I saw his finger tighten on the trigger.

"Yes," Geoff acknowledged, "I did bumble a bit. You really almost confessed to me when we visited your home, didn't you? Communism, you said, was gobbling up country after country. The West hadn't much time left since impending protection from nuclear attack would also remove our last powerful retaliatory weapon. We had to rediscover *and export* capitalism. Jim Strong's election would, perhaps, precipitate the rediscovering, but exportation would have to wait. You'd already said, however, that we couldn't afford to wait even a little while. Strong wasn't a hawk. Even if he were, the doves in Congress would override him. You were telling me that, in your opinion, a communist victory over the United States was inevitable. Political flip-flopping is one of your trademarks, and you jolly well wanted to wind up on the winning side. Let me guess how it would happen by putting together other elements of what you said. Moles living in this country would start raising havoc. A guerilla army would invade from Mexico. If I remember my social studies correctly, as President *pro tempore* of the Senate, you're fourth in line for the presidency. The men above you would die and you'd refuse to act against the invasion. Isn't that substantially correct?"

"Very nearly," Billings acknowledged. "You have your moments, Weston. Those moments, however, now come to an end!"

Weston, who'd placed his thumb in the shoe, made no attempt to duck as the shot was fired. At the very instant before the explosion, however, Billings's jaw went slack. The bullet skimmed past my partner's head and splintered the solid wood front of the Speaker's desk. Billings sat looking straight ahead with the lifeless stare I'd seen on the faces of three-day-dead fish. His wife, seated to my right, broke into hysterical sobbing and buried her face in her hands. Meanwhile, pandemonium broke out everywhere and the Speaker dented his desk with gavel blows while Col. Claypool stepped over and disarmed the flaccid suspect. Geoff held up his arm for quiet.

"Ladies and gentlemen," he urged, "please remain seated and quiet down. The next few minutes are critical and I'm going to have to explain the situation to you quickly now, or thousands of Americans may yet die."

His words took immediate effect and the noisy confusion subsided.

"Let me start by saying this," Geoff resumed when he had everyone's attention. "The murderer has not been disabled since he was only partially here to begin with. I know that sounds preposterous, but it's true nonetheless. Do you see this?" He held the shoe opening forward so everyone could peer inside at a small box with a button on it which he'd concealed there. "This is a transmitter rigged to automatically activate a powerful radio jamming station set up on the grounds outside the Capitol. Thanks to Col. Claypool virtually every radio and television transmission in this city is now totally disrupted. That is the reason Desmond Billings looks as he does.

"Briefly stated, Senator Billings had inoperative cancer. His wife's company was perfecting a device to enable direct communication between computers and the human brain. It must be some kind of converter changing digital electrical impulses from the computer to electrochemical impulses receivable by the brain's analog thought system. Lillian, or perhaps Desmond himself, had an inspirational flash born of desperation. Why not use the device to record Desmond's conscious and subconscious memory on computer tape, then remove that portion of his brain around the tumor and replace it with an interfacing unit linked by transmitter to the computer? He'd still have access to his full memory. In fact, he'd have a better memory than before since the computer makes no distinction between conscious and unconscious. I realized that was what must have happened as soon as I read Billings's school records. He'd nearly failed in elementary school despite good attendance and good behavior. Where was that photographic memory then? Obviously it didn't exist. It had to be, therefore, that secret operation in a hospital owned by a bionics research company which had made the difference. The conclusion was obvious—particularly when one considered the electronic theft from our bank account.

"Unfortunately the communication between man and machine was a matter of give and take. The computer could not forget, neither did it remember only facts. It also remembered motives. Its motivation led it to feed its facts where and when it wanted. The man slowly became the machine. Perhaps I should say Billings came to be possessed by the soulless contraption. One of the Senator's strongest drives was survival. All the information the computer had indicated the West would eventually lose. Therefore, it sided with the communists in their 'Operation Fruit Basket.' That title is, incidentally, an obvious allusion to the early Soviet boast that once Central America and Mexico were gone, America would fall like 'ripe fruit' into socialist hands. Throughout my investigation I've had the feeling we were up against an utterly inhuman foe who used people as pawns and planned contingency moves several steps ahead. That is, in reality, what was happening. The computer must now assume that Billings is dead and be starting a contingency plan. I think I know what it is."

He fished a piece of paper from his pocket and held it up for the audience.

"This Library of Congress stacks pass was used by one of Billings's men. From the very first day I wondered why. Then it dawned on me. The library was the one sure link between the killer and virtually every important government official. The library was also so immense that books with fictitious call numbers could remain there indefinitely without being detected. Furthermore, guards didn't check books being brought into the building, only those going out.

"If my theory is correct, right now someone is submitting call slips across the street designed to send certain volumes to loan division, then through the underground tube and eventually to your offices. Other books would hurry on their way to the President himself, the Vice President behind me, and to every member of the Cabinet. In short, these books, bearing some sort of lethal cargo, would kill everyone empowered to govern in the President's absence and the Congress which is alone empowered to declare war.

"At the same time, the computer is now telephoning the terrorist network with which Billings has ingratiated himself. Sabateurs in this country are about to strike pre-selected targets. They'll have a rough time of it, however, because most of those targets are now being defended. The booby-trapped books won't reach their destinations either because the gentleman who deposits the slips will be summarily arrested and the books requested by the slips disposed of. As to the computer which is evidently hidden in the hill behind Billings's house . . . . Well, we'll let it operate just long enough to set its contingency plan into motion so that the revolutionary network in this country can be completely exposed. President Guerrero will obviously want to alert his army because the invasion of Mexico from the south is also scheduled to begin now.

"Meanwhile, you gentlemen will have to enact your own legislation to meet the emergency and support Mexico's defense. After that, it would be nice if you'd finally take steps to control your borders so this doesn't all happen again. Now, are there any questions?"

The response was deafening as senators and representatives vied with each other to be heard. Hands shot up and waved for recognition. The Speaker's gavel fell again and again but couldn't be heard for the din. Words meshed with words and produced a roar I've seldom heard even at soccer matches. Only Senator Billings sat aloof from the clamor staring straight ahead. Tears were streaming down Lillian's cheeks and I could see her speaking softly amidst the bedlam. My lip reading isn't the best, but I believe her words were, "I didn't know. I didn't know."

EPILOG

Bluebirds and sparrows seemed to serenade us from the trees, and a brown squirrel scampered across the sidewalk to our table, begging crumbs for his round tummy.

"It seems so peaceful," Cathleen Strong declared as she looked across the street at the park-like Capitol grounds. "Who'd ever think that murder could take place in a setting like this . . . that Jim could have been struck dead just a few feet away."

Clyde unwrapped his submarine sandwich and looked critically at its contents.

"Yeah," he agreed, "and who ever thought that when Taylor told us he'd spring for lunch, we'd end up like tourists stuffing our faces on a Library of Congress bench?"

Weston translated the slang parts for Paloma and she looked most sweetly indignant.

"I think it's really nice here," she defended. "It's just like Chepultapec Park. What's more I don't have to worry about Geoff dating me just to trap the criminal." She gave him a playful sidelong glance. "And the . . . how do you call them? . . . hoggies are delicious."

Even Pollard had to laugh at that.

"Hoagies," Weston corrected her with a chuckle.

"New York hoagies," I added. "They're the best in the world—if local propaganda can be believed."

"It's too bad," she noted more soberly, "that daddy couldn't be here to try them. The country needs him home, though, very badly. It's good to know that the communist army is retreating south from Puebla."

"Yes, it is," I concurred, "and that only three power plants and two dams have been blown up so far by saboteurs in this country."

190

"What bothers me," Pollard reflected, "is that the first 'human computer' decided we don't stand a chance against the commies in the long run. That thought's unsettling."

Geoff took a bite off the end of his sandwich.

"Don't get too jittery," he advised with very poor diction. "Remember that that same computer thought it had killed John and me several times. Computers are, after all, horribly limited and utterly earthbound. They're incapable of integrating either hope or faith into their reasoning. By rights John and I should be dead now. We should have gotten on that plane, but someone was praying for us. That satchel full of explosives that was tossed into our flat should have blown our heads off, but we were praying inside. By all the rules of earthbound logic, the computer won and we lost. By all the rules of faith, the contraption didn't stand a chance. By purely human reasoning, things don't look very rosy for the West either, since people can always be induced to revolt against those who have more than they do if they're offered a cut from the spoils. At the same time, I find it hard to believe God would let the lamp of freedom go out entirely, unless that's what it takes to prove the fraudulent nature of communist promises and destroy the system entirely. Then the loss would be worth it, I guess."

"How do you suppose," Paloma remarked thoughtfully, "Senator Billings smuggled that pistol past all the metal detectors?"

"Probably," Pollard declared, "by concealing it in a compartment he'd built into his chrome-plated chair. The shoes are more puzzling to me. Hundreds of congressmen wore them through the sensors without raising so much as a buzz."

"That's no problem at all," I explained. "I saw a cowboy walk through without challenge in boots that must have contained half a pound of steel arch supports. The detectors are probably set to pass metal in certain areas of the body."

I opened my hoagie and spooned on extra mustard.

"What baffles me," I admitted, "is why Desmond Billings chatted with us so freely when Geoff and I visited. His comments about one of our previous cases showing scientists that there were moral research limits really sounds like high irony now. Did the computer actually feel emotion? Was it toying with us?"

"I rather think," Weston concluded, "that the situation was reminiscent of those Scriptural accounts where demon-possessed men came to Jesus and were liberated. In moments of ebbing demonic control, they may have struggled desperately for relief. In the same way, the human part of Billings was probably crying out for help, but the machine part responded by overloading his brain. Consider that Billings was right-handed and, therefore, left-brained. The operation on the dominant lobe assured computer mastery, but every now and then the machine evidently had to shock the subverted and weaker human side into submission. Remember how the man contorted in a pain spasm while he talked? Billings probably showed enough of the same behavior before Jim Strong to arouse his suspicions."

Geoff nodded toward the lady who'd hired us. "Your husband, Mrs. Strong, was quite a man. Even that volume on biological warfare he had the librarians hunting for turned out to be prophetic, considering what was found on those booby-trapped books. I have a feeling that if he'd lived a little longer, the case would have been solved and you'd have saved the cost of our fee."

Cathleen shook her head, then adjusted her glasses which had slid down the ridge of her nose.

"I wish he had lived," she declared, "but I doubt he was all that close. Thank you, though, for trying to give me the best possible memories. Rest assured I don't begrudge you even a penny. Now that you've unmasked my husband's killer, I believe I can put some of the pain from Jim's death behind me and rest content knowing that someday we'll be reunited. You know, you've probably saved our country, Mr. Weston. I

192

hear there's even talk of awarding you the Congressional Medal of Honor."

My partner's face reddened slightly, but not from sunburn. "That, madam, is, I believe, a military decoration and I'm no soldier. Let's leave the medals for the heroes."

Cathleen eyed him gravely. "There have been exceptions made, Mr. Weston, to sometimes grant a civilian military honors . . . when that civilian is truly exceptional."

"That's all he needs!" Pollard broke in while waving his sandwich under my nose for emphasis. "The man is already impossible. He's an honorary citizen, a member of the FBI. That bank account business has been straightened out, so he's well-heeled. He's going to gloat for hours when he finds out my wife wants to talk with him and John about the Messiah. Like a fool I went and blabbed about our little arguments. You make him an official hero, and his head'll grow so big he won't be able to cram it through the Concorde door to fly home."

Paloma impulsively clasped Geoff's hand as it rested on the table. "He doesn't need any medal," she informed us with a twinkle in her eye. "He's already my hero."

Just then the sun peeked out from behind a cloud and the third finger on her left hand glittered with rainbow-tinted fire. I hadn't noticed the ring before. Neither, evidently, had her Secret Service chaperone seated at the next bench. I saw him smile. Come to think of it, I believe I may have grinned a might myself. So Geoff had finally accepted Paloma's notion that if the Lord brought them together He would also protect them!

"When," I asked impulsively, "are you two planning to walk the aisle?"

Paloma positively beamed. "In about a year, as soon as my father's term of office expires. Papa's afraid a Protestant wedding any sooner would weaken his party leadership and aid the rebels."

"I fear," Weston added, "that the President and I have had our first domestic disagreement on that point since I'm not one to accommodate prejudice on any account. A delayed marriage with presidential blessing, however, will do far more to further the evangelical cause in Mexico than an argument followed by an elopement. It's rather nicer, too, don't you think?"

"My," I noted in mock wonder. "You're developing diplomatic understanding! She suits you well, Geoff, but don't let her polish smooth too many of your rough edges. We won't recognize you."

Paloma laughed and squeezed his hand. "I do not think that will be a problem for you, unless you get married before we do and move away. Geoff's buying the, how do you call it, 'brownstone,' in London so that you can live in the second floor apartment while we stay downstairs."

"Or," Weston amended, "the other way around. We'll decide that later."

Paloma leaned forward conspiratorially. "At any rate, we'll be seeing each other every day, so you aren't likely to ever find Geoff unrecognizable, even if I sew him a thousand disguises."

"How jolly!" I responded. "Imagine wearing costumes and bulletproof jackets tailored by a professional designer. We're certainly coming up in the world."

Weston nodded happily. "That's not the half of it, John. She wants to help us out from time to time on our cases. I believe that observations from a woman's perspective could prove invaluable in our line of endeavor. What do you think?"

"I think," I wisecracked, "that I'm about to faint dead away in surprise. I also applaud your change of heart. It's about time Sleuths Ltd. became a little less limited."

"This is a great day for the firm," Geoff agreed. He paused to scowl. " . . . in every way but one."

Pollard jacked his eyebrows up a few millimeters. "Meaning?"

"Well," Weston complained, "I don't think it was cricket of that local landlord chap to refuse to return our security deposit. After all, he *is* insured, and it's not our fault somebody burned down the building. We were just lounging about . . . . "

The rest of his comments were drowned out by our laughter. Some things might have changed, but inside he was the same old Geoff.